Untamed Heart

Look for these titles by
Ally Blue

Now Available:

Bay City Paranormal Investigations Series:
Oleander House (Book 1)
What Hides Inside (Book 2)
Twilight (Book 3)
Closer (Book 4)
An Inner Darkness (Book 5)

Print Anthologies:
Hearts from The Ashes
Temperature's Rising

Willow Bend
Love's Evolution
Eros Rising
Catching a Buzz
Fireflies
The Happy Onion

Untamed Heart

Ally Blue

A SAMHAIN PUBLISHING, LTD. publication.

Samhain Publishing, Ltd.
577 Mulberry Street, Suite 1520
Macon, GA 31201
www.samhainpublishing.com

Untamed Heart
Copyright © 2008 by Ally Blue
Print ISBN: 978-1-60504-027-1
Digital ISBN: 1-59998-881-X

Editing by Sasha Knight
Cover by Anne Cain

First Samhain Publishing, Ltd. electronic publication: February 2008
First Samhain Publishing, Ltd. print publication: December 2008

Dedication

As always, to the girls of the J_A_W_breakers for sticking with me through the whole creation process. Also, to Patrick Wolf for the inspirational soundtrack, videos and wardrobe.

Prologue

Frank Gold never locked his doors.

Leon Fisher, who'd been watching Frank's house from the park across the street for the last week, was relieved by this fact. It meant entering the house after Frank was asleep that night would be a piece of cake.

In any other circumstances, Leon would've been annoyed. He rather enjoyed a challenge, and what challenge did an unlocked door present?

Of course, finding the man hadn't presented much of a challenge either. A few well-placed threats, enough money in the right pockets, and Leon had all the information he needed. The many aliases hadn't fooled him any. It was easy enough to put together the puzzle pieces of Frank's history.

Leon had lost the capacity to be surprised by the incompetence of law enforcement ages ago, or he might've been shocked by the sheer number of crimes Frank Gold had committed over the years without ever seeing the inside of a prison. But then again, getting away with murder—literally— was far easier than most people thought. All it took was cast-iron balls and a staggering amount of arrogance. Most serial killers, at least in Leon's experience, had that in spades.

Not that it would help Frank tonight, Leon thought, smiling grimly behind the magazine he was pretending to read. No lock could've kept him out. Frank Gold had signed his own death sentence the day he murdered Ted.

Which, of course, was why Leon was currently relieved rather than annoyed. Sure, he loved a challenge. This time, however, all he wanted was revenge.

The hours passed, and the park emptied as the mild afternoon faded into the hard chill of a January evening. At six o'clock, Frank Gold left his house and walked briskly down the street. Leon knew where he was going—Hoffman's Deli, three blocks down. Frank went to Hoffman's every day at six p.m., bought a roast beef sandwich with horseradish sauce and chips, and took it home to eat.

Folding his magazine, Leon rose, picked up his bag and headed the other way, to the Thai place around the corner. Ted had loved Thai food. Leon had never cared for it before, but lately he found himself developing a taste for it.

Much later, Leon sat under the big oak in the park and watched the light from Frank's TV flicker in his living room window. Shielding his watch with one leather-gloved hand, Leon hit the button to light up the digital display. Nine thirty. In half an hour, Frank would turn off the TV and go to bed. Without locking his doors.

He followed the same routine every single night, which had made it ridiculously easy for Leon to lay his plans. Yes, it would have been more satisfying if his target didn't behave as though he actually wanted someone to walk into his house and kill him. But that was secondary. Mostly, Leon looked forward to watching Frank Gold suffer and die.

Leon waited another hour after the light went off in Frank's house before moving out from under the tree. Black bag in hand, he strolled across the street and into the yellow glow of Frank's porch light. He didn't bother to check and see if anyone was watching, just walked briskly up to the door and opened it. If you acted like you had a God-given right to be there, he'd found, you could walk in practically anywhere and people wouldn't question it.

The hinges squeaked when Leon entered the house and shut the door behind him, but the faint sound wasn't enough to wake Frank. His bedroom was in the back of the single-story building, and he always kept the door shut. Leon had learned this by climbing the backyard fence and watching Frank prepare for bed four nights in a row.

Those nights, it had taken all of Leon's strength to resist the urge to kick in the window, leap into the austere little room and beat Frank Gold's head against the floor until it burst like an egg.

Such a death was too quick and easy for the bastard.

Leon's fingers clenched on the handle of his equipment bag. In a few minutes, the contents of that bag would make Frank Gold wish he'd never targeted Ted Stevenson as a victim in his torture-and-murder game.

Silence. Dread. Ropes and blood and blue eyes...

Leon shook himself, forcing back the images and the rage which always went with them. *Not now,* he ordered himself as he stalked down the short hallway to Frank's bedroom. *Save it for Frank.*

Twitching his jacket aside, Leon drew his gun and flicked the safety off. The suppressor was already in place over the muzzle. He slipped his bag over the wrist of his left hand, opened the door to Frank's bedroom and aimed the gun directly at the salt-and-pepper head faintly visible on the pillow. The bed was situated with the wooden-slat headboard against the wall to Leon's right. Frank lay on his right side, putting his back to the door.

His unlocked bedroom door.

Either suicidal, or stupid. Not that it mattered. He was dead either way.

Moving with the speed and accuracy of long practice, Leon crossed to the bed, dropped the bag on the floor and jammed the gun's muzzle against the base of Frank's skull. He heard the sharp intake of breath when Frank woke, and felt a surge of fierce satisfaction.

"Roll onto your stomach," Leon ordered, in the cold, crisp voice he used for face-to-face kills. "Hands behind your head, fingers laced. I'm sure you know the drill."

Frank did exactly as Leon said, rolling onto his front and lacing his fingers behind his head. "Am I under arrest?"

Leon had to laugh at that. "I'm not a cop, Frank." Whipping the handcuffs from his pocket, Leon cuffed Frank's wrists to the headboard. "Roll onto your back again."

"How? You've restrained my wrists so that I—"

"Just fucking do it." Leon backed up enough that Frank wouldn't be able to kick him. "Now. Before I lose my patience."

Frank obediently turned over, much less gracefully than before. Leon waited. He wanted to look Frank in the face. Wanted to watch his pain. Wanted to watch the life drain from his eyes.

On his back again, Frank stared at Leon without a trace of fear on his round, plain face. His wrists were twisted at a painful-looking angle, but he didn't seem to notice, which just made Leon angrier.

Wait, said the cold-blooded assassin in Leon's mind. The part of him which had killed countless men and women over the years without regret or remorse, earning himself a very comfortable living. *Anger makes you careless. Remember, he's killed before. Ted wasn't his first victim, and wouldn't have been his last. Neutralize the danger to yourself first. Then get as angry as you like.*

Forcing back the fury boiling inside him, Leon squatted on the floor, opened the bag and took out a roll of twine. "Feet together," he ordered. "Knees straight, legs flat on the bed."

Frank did as he was told, but Leon felt the weight of his prisoner's calculating gaze. When he set the gun on the floor and leaned over to bind Frank's ankles, he was prepared for the attempted kick in the face. He caught Frank's bare foot easily, pressed it beside the other with all the weight of his muscular body and wound the twine around both feet from toes to ankles. Frank's blue cotton pajamas bunched under the string. If the bonds were tighter than was strictly necessary, well, Frank could consider that his punishment for trying to kick.

"I take it you aren't going to rape me," Frank observed as Leon secured his feet to the bottom of the bedframe. "Considering the position I find myself in, that is."

"Believe me, Frank, your ass holds no appeal for me whatsoever." Rising to his feet, Leon turned on the bedside lamp and inspected his handiwork with a critical eye. The bonds would need to hold firm through a great deal of struggling. He tugged on the length of twine running from Frank's ankles to the bedframe and nodded, satisfied. "Are you disappointed?"

"No. Although if my preferences leaned in that direction, I might be. You're a very attractive man, you know, in a brutish sort of way." Tilting his head, Frank gave Leon a curious look. "Wait. You're Ted Stevenson's lover, aren't you? I saw your picture in his house." Frank grinned in a way that turned Leon's stomach. "He screamed for you, you know. Over and over again. Begging for you to save him. My God, it was magnificent, the way he screamed."

Frank could've been lying. Probably was, actually. But the damage was done.

The flashback hit Leon like it always did, swift and shocking as a bullet to the brain. His jaw clenched, fingers convulsing as the hated images punched through to his conscious mind...

Key in the lock. Door pushed open. Calling Ted, expecting his lover to saunter up and greet him with a kiss, as he usually did after Leon came home from an assignment.

No answer this time. No music from Ted's CD player, no smells of dinner cooking. Lights on all over, but no sound.

Up the stairs, cautious now. Instincts on high alert. Gun drawn, safety off. Hands steady in spite of his fear. His hands never shake. Never.

Bedroom door's closed. Cold metal of the doorknob, turning, swinging the door open. And there's Ted, naked, tied spread-eagle to the four-poster bed they'd bought when they moved in together. Skin flayed from muscle, muscle ripped from bone, abdomen laid open, intestines spilling out. Blood everywhere. Dead eyes staring at him, still blue as the summer sky.

Leon came to himself with a start. Heart racing, he forced his blank mask into place and managed to hold Frank's gaze without any apparent reaction. But his hands trembled, and he knew Frank saw.

He hated the flashbacks. Hated being forced to relive it. To see the man he'd loved more than life itself gutted like an animal.

The coroner said Ted had been tortured for hours before he died. That the person who did it must've broken in not long after Leon left on assignment. The worst part was, Ted had still been alive when his killer cut him open. That had been even

14

harder for Leon to bear than knowing he could've prevented it if he'd been home.

Frank laughed. "You try so hard to be cold, but I see the fire inside you. You want to torture me, and you tell yourself it's because of what I did to Ted, but it isn't, is it?"

For a second, time seemed to stop. Staring into Frank's strangely bright eyes, Leon saw a reflection of himself. What he would become if he let himself do this. Because Frank was right. Leon didn't want to torture him for Ted. He wanted to do it for himself, because he knew it would feel so fucking sweet. And then what would make him any different from Frank Gold?

Bending down, Leon placed his bag on the floor. He wouldn't be needing the equipment he'd brought after all.

He picked up his gun, paced to the head of the bed and traced the rounded angles of Frank's jawline with the pistol's barrel. "I think you have a death wish, Frank. Well, tonight, I'm your fucking fairy godfather."

Frank's eyes widened, and Leon wasn't sure if what he saw there was terror or relief.

Not that it mattered. He pressed the muzzle of the gun to Frank's temple and pulled the trigger.

A soft *thunk* sounded as the bullet tore through Frank's skull. Blood, brains and bits of bone splattered the other side of the bed, speckling the floor and the nearby wall as well. A wet spot spread across the front of Frank's pajama pants, the tang of urine filling the air as Frank's bladder let go. Frank's face, still more or less intact, went slack. The weird lustful shine faded from his eyes, and there he lay, just a dead man in plain blue cotton pajamas, with lines on his face and the beginnings of a double chin.

Leon stared at the limp body, waiting for the hard knot which had been in his gut since Ted died to unwind. Waiting for the endless, gnawing pain of loss to go away.

Nothing changed. Ted was still gone, and it didn't hurt any less than it had before Leon's gun blew Frank Gold's head apart.

With nothing to keep him there, Leon turned his back on the man he'd just killed and left the room. He used Frank's phone to call 911 and report a dead body at 1447 Walnut Street before walking out of the house.

Outside, he tilted his head back and stared up into the night sky. Low-hanging clouds and streetlight glare obscured the stars. Leon drew a deep breath. The air was freezing cold, burning his lungs. If it was just a little sharper, he figured, it could almost cut the empty ache from his chest.

He wished he was able to believe there was some sort of harmony in the world. That the bad things were balanced by good ones.

Ted had believed that. Leon couldn't. Life had taught him there was no such thing.

In the distance, sirens began to wail, coming closer. Picking up his pace, Leon turned down a narrow, unlit side street and vanished into the darkness.

Chapter One

Los Angeles, Leon thought, improved a great deal when seen through a whiskey haze. It softened the harsh glare of the afternoon sun on car windshields and lent a mellow glow to the cluster of grimy, graffitti-covered buildings. He raised his glass to the smog-shrouded city in a silent toast, then tossed back the last of the amber liquid. It burned its way down his throat to warm his gut for a few wonderful minutes.

Lately, it took more and more whiskey to keep the cold inside him at bay. He recognized that, saw himself losing his edge, but couldn't bring himself to care.

You're depressed, the shrink he'd been forced to see had insisted at their session that morning, crossing his legs and folding his plump, soft hands atop his plump, soft knee. *Turning to alcohol in such times is quite common. Nothing to be ashamed of, and nothing we can't work through with a bit of effort, eh?*

Leon snorted at the memory. He'd asked the self-satisfied prick if finding one's lover cut open by a serial killer was also "quite common", and if offing the murdering bastard might be something they could "work through".

Unsurprisingly, the man hadn't been able to answer either question. Instead, he'd gaped like a fish for a moment before informing Leon that the session was over and to please see his secretary to schedule next week's appointment. He'd berated Leon for the umpteenth time about not taking his meds and shooed him out of the office.

"Fuck you," Leon growled, gesturing at the gridlocked traffic four stories below with his empty glass. "What the fuck do you know? Pompous asshole."

Maybe he was being unfair, but he didn't think so. Dr. Smith—not his real name, of course—was as deeply entrenched in Big Brother's cruel embrace as Leon was. He should be used to the ravings of fucked-up killers-for-hire by now.

Leon had "forgotten" to make another appointment when he left the office. He wondered if anyone would notice.

"Drunk already? Sloppy, Mr. Fisher. Very sloppy."

Jones. Damn her. Grimacing, Leon stood and leaned on the balcony railing. "What the fuck are you doing here?" He didn't turn to look at her, and he didn't ask how she'd gotten in. People like her went wherever they wanted, whenever they wanted.

Behind Leon, heels clicked on bare concrete. "This place is a cesspit," Jones observed, laying her manicured fingers on the railing. "I understand why you wanted to move after...the incident, but really, you have better taste than this."

The incident. Almost a year after Ted was butchered, Jones still called it that. Leon hated it with a purple passion. He would've hit her, if he didn't know for a fact that she could kill him before he could blink.

"What do you want, Jones?" He lifted his glass, remembered it was empty and scowled. "Do you have an assignment for me?"

"What do you think?"

"Let's see." Setting his glass on the little plastic table, Leon turned around and leaned his butt against the railing. "In the last decade, you and your mysterious bosses haven't gone more than a couple of months without giving me a new hit. It's been six months since I killed that fucking waste of space Frank Gold, and there hasn't been an assignment in all that time. I haven't even seen your butt-ugly face since you came and threatened me into seeing that fucking idiotic psychiatrist last month. I'm thinking you're not here to give me a hit."

"You always were a smart man." Jones turned to face him, her dark-skinned—and not at all ugly—face as expressionless as ever. "You used to be the best hit man in the business. That's why my colleagues and I made certain you were not implicated in Frank Gold's murder. But ever since the incident, you've been unstable. Dangerous."

Leon laughed. "Wouldn't be much of an assassin if I wasn't dangerous."

Jones' eyes flashed in a rare display of irritation. "I'll be blunt, Mr. Fisher. My superiors are at the end of their patience. Either you shape up, or you will be let go."

He knew what that meant, and it had nothing to do with two weeks' notice or severance pay. "I'm seeing your fucking shrink. What else do you want me to do?"

"Dr. Smith tells me you did not make a follow-up appointment this morning and have not been taking the medication he prescribed." Red nails tapped on the balcony rail, the only sign of how much Leon tried Jones' patience. "Since you refuse to work with Dr. Smith, we have decided to work with you instead."

Leon's interest was piqued in spite of himself. He crossed his arms and cocked his head sideways. "What's that mean, exactly?"

"It means that your last chance to get yourself back on

track will be more in line with your antisocial tendencies than our previous efforts have been." Reaching into her dark gray suit jacket, she pulled out a sheet of paper and held it out to him. "Your travel information."

Travel? Leon snatched the paper from Jones' hand. He skimmed it, then threw it on the floor. "No."

"Yes." Jones picked up the paper, walked through the open sliding glass door into his tiny dining area and set the paper on the table next to a pile of dirty bowls. "You leave tomorrow morning."

He followed her inside, simmering with rage. The anger chased away the icy numbness he'd lived in for months and was therefore rather welcome. "I'm not going to fucking *Alaska.* No."

"Your flight to Juneau leaves at ten a.m.," she continued as if she hadn't heard him. "One of our people will pick you up at seven to drive you to LAX. A private charter plane will meet you at the airport in Juneau and fly you to our property."

Leon wanted to tell her to fuck off, that they couldn't make him do this. Because they couldn't, really. If he chose not to get on that plane in the morning, no force in this world could make him. Of course, he'd find himself on the business end of another assassin's gun in short order if he refused. And in spite of everything, in spite of the black despair blanketing him these days, he wasn't ready to die.

"Who'd you pay off to let me carry my gun on?" he asked, forcing his voice to remain calm. "Security's fucking brutal these days. I do *not* want to end up with a screener who's not in your pocket."

"I haven't paid off anyone."

He raised his eyebrows at her. "You know I don't like to put my gun in my checked luggage, Jones. That pistol's a custom job. No one touches it but me."

Jones pinned him with a baleful look. "You will not be taking your weapon. I'd be happy to take it with me, if you like. Considering the neighborhood you've chosen to live in, leaving it in this apartment might not be the best option."

No weapon. Fuck. The prospect made Leon's skin twitch. He hadn't been without his custom-made .22 Wilson combat pistol since the first time he'd touched it. It would be like leaving a piece of his body behind.

He would've argued if he thought it would do any good, but he knew it wouldn't. Either he'd fly to bum-fuck Alaska without his beloved gun, or he'd die with it in his hand.

Not much of a choice. He'd never hated Jones and her faceless bosses more than he did right then.

He gritted his teeth. "Fuck you, Jones."

"You will be staying at a private safe house outside Juneau, in the borders of the Tongass National Forest. The house is owned by my superiors for just such instances, and is fully staffed. You will even find clothing there to fit you, suitable to the current weather conditions." She gave him a cool look. "You are not the first of your sort to require a bit of quiet time alone to consider his situation."

Your tax dollars at work. Leon's lips curled into a bitter smile. Though Jones had never said so, he'd guessed long ago that his assignments—and his massive paychecks—came from a shadow agency of the U.S. government.

"Fine, so I go to this place of yours." Leon plopped into a chair, picked up a none-too-clean plastic tumbler and poured a generous amount of whiskey from the open bottle on the table. "What then? How long are you leaving me there, and just what the fuck am I supposed to do to keep myself busy? I don't guess this place has a bar?"

"No bar. You hardly need to pickle yourself further." Jones surveyed Leon's dirty apartment with unveiled disgust. "As far as entertainment, there is a plasma screen television, DVDs, a gym and a full library. Or, you could always venture outdoors. The property has miles of well-maintained trails, and a private lake with a pier and a canoe. As long as you stay on the trails, or in the confines of the lake, you should be safe enough."

Leon scraped a bit of dried egg off the table. "What's to stop me from taking off? Just disappearing into the woods?"

Jones' laugh came as a surprise. Leon had never heard her laugh before. He stared at her.

"You will be watched, naturally," she said, ignoring his bald-faced shock. "Mr. Fisher, you have many talents, but wilderness survival is not one of them. The only way in or out of our compound is by private plane. There are no roads other than the one from our private runway to the house, and the forest is very thick. If you tried to hike out, you'd be hopelessly lost within an hour." She smiled, looking vaguely reptilian for a moment. "I will return in three months to bring you back. If you are not at the house, my people—who *are* skilled survivalists— will find you, wherever you are, and neutralize you. Are we clear?"

"Crystal." Leon took a deep swallow of whiskey, glaring at Jones over the rim of the tumbler. "Why don't you go away now, and let me get drunk in peace?"

Jones held out one slim hand. "Your weapon, please."

It was all Leon could do not to draw down on the cunt. The insistent desire to live made him reach into the custom leather holster at the small of his back, pull his pistol out and lay it in Jones' hand.

"I hate you, you fucking bitch."

"The feeling, I assure you, is entirely mutual." Jones tucked

Leon's gun into one of the thousands of magic pockets she always seemed to have inside her suit jacket. "Three months, Mr. Fisher. I sincerely hope the change of scenery improves your state of mind."

Leon didn't answer, didn't look up as Jones walked out of his apartment and shut the door with a soft snick. He emptied the tumbler in one gulp, shuddering as the alcohol seared his stomach.

"Of all the places in the fucking world, it had to be Alaska," he mumbled, frowning. "Not London, or New York, or Berlin. No. Fucking *Alaska*."

Just me, alone with the memories and the nightmares. No liquor, no drugs. No escape.

Leon pushed to his feet, swaying as the last shot of liquor hit him like a load of bricks. He picked up the whiskey bottle and staggered back out onto the balcony. "Here's to L.A.," he called, holding up the bottle. "I hate this fucking shithole, but it's better than Alaska."

He put the mouth of the bottle to his lips and drank as the drug dealers who'd emerged onto the balcony next door answered his toast with an equally scathing one of their own. The city blurred around him, the bottle falling from his numb fingers as the white plastic of the cheap patio table rushed up to smack him in the face. He drifted in an alcoholic stupor, grateful for the brief respite from the emptiness eating at him like a cancer.

There would be no such refuge in Alaska. The thought terrified him beyond all reason.

"God, I'm fucked," he muttered, and passed out.

Chapter Two

By the time the tiny private plane achieved a hair-raising landing on the impossibly small strip of tarmac, the monstrous pain in Leon's head had faded to a dull throb. Thank whatever powers existed for airport bars and the miniature liquor bottles on airplane beverage carts.

Jones wouldn't approve, but fuck her. She wasn't here, and if she was he'd cheerfully tell her to bite his ass. That's what she got for booking him on a commercial flight.

He'd woken up that morning still in the cracked plastic chair on the balcony, his last whiskey bottle lying empty between his feet and the great exalted mother of all hangovers pounding in his skull. With nothing in his apartment to soothe the headache or quiet the waves of nausea, he'd been forced to settle for a little hair of the dog, bought at the airport bar. Not ideal, but better than nothing. At least he could face the vehemently bright afternoon head-on—albeit through dark sunglasses—without flinching.

"There's clear weather forecast for the next week," the pilot said as she opened the passenger door for Leon. "You're a lucky bastard, getting that long a stretch here without rain in July."

"Yeah. Lucky, that's me." Leon climbed out of the plane, his duffle bag slung over his shoulder. "So how do I get to this house?"

"The jeep should be on the way to meet us." The pilot— Jennifer? Jessica? something like that—smiled at him. "So, Mr. Thompson. You must be pretty important to get invited here. The owner's a real recluse, I hear."

"Do you really." Walking away from the plane, Leon surveyed his surroundings. Thick, verdant forest pressed in on all sides, rising up the slopes of nearby snowcapped mountains. Beautiful terrain, but hostile. *Looks like I really am stuck here. Dammit.*

And why's that so terrible? a little voice inside him whispered. *You hated L.A. You only lived there in the first place because Ted loved it. Maybe this'll be better. Maybe it'll be good for you to be someplace different. Someplace away from all those memories.*

More like someplace where there was nothing to drown out the memories. Leon wrinkled his nose. He must be losing it, if his own brain was talking to him like that fucking asshole psychiatrist.

"Mr. Thompson?"

Leon shook his head and turned back to the pilot. She looked nervous. "Mr. Thompson, are you all right? I called your name like five times and you didn't answer."

Fucking aliases. It had been far too long since he'd been visible enough to need an alias. He wasn't used to it.

"Sorry, just thinking." He forced a smile, and almost laughed at the expression of relief on the young woman's face. Hell, he wasn't *that* intimidating. "What is it?"

"Nothing much. I was just going to tell you that if you go walking in the woods around here, be careful. There's bears." She leaned closer, excitement lighting her brown eyes. "I've heard there's been Bigfoot sightings out here too."

Leon managed not to roll his eyes, but it was a near thing.

Never piss off the driver, that was his motto. If this little girl ended up being the one to fly him back out of here, he didn't want her mad at him for scoffing at her gullibility.

"Okay. I'll keep that in mind, thanks." Leon silently congratulated himself for sounding pleasant instead of sarcastic.

A sly expression slid into the girl's eyes. "You know, I'm a freelance pilot. I make my own schedule. If you want to go clubbing in Juneau, have Carl at the house radio me. I'll be glad to show you around."

Leon bit back a groan. Tempting as the thought of clubbing in the city was, there was no way he could get away with it without Jones finding out. Hell, for all he knew, Jennifer or Jessica or whatever the fuck her name was had instructions to proposition him and rat him out if he took her up on it.

"Thanks, but I'm here to get away from the club scene for a while," he lied. "Just looking for a little peace and quiet, you know? Time to think."

Yeah, time to think. Plenty of time to get so lost in your own fucked-up head you'll never get out again.

A spark of panic fluttered in Leon's belly. He stamped it out. He hadn't wanted to come here, but he'd been given no choice. Now that he was here, all he could do was suck it up and deal with it. He would find a way to keep the nightmares and flashbacks at bay if it fucking killed him.

The implications in that thought were not lost on him. The fact that it actually seemed like a comforting prospect sometimes scared him.

The rumble of an engine sounded somewhere behind Leon. He turned to see a mud-splattered Jeep emerge from an opening in the trees and bounce across the narrow strip of grass between the forest and the tarmac. The Jeep came to a halt a few feet away. The door opened, and a man in jeans, work boots and a leather jacket hopped out.

"Mr. Thompson?" the man said, turning a keen blue-eyed gaze to Leon. "I'm Carl Black, head groundskeeper at the lake house. Can I take your bag?"

"I got it." Ignoring the man's outstretched hand, Leon strolled to the Jeep, opened the passenger side door and slung his bag into the backseat. "Could we head on to the house now? I'm not feeling too well. I'd like to lie down."

Pilot-woman's expression softened in sympathy. Carl Black raised a skeptical eyebrow, as if he could read the previous evening's whiskey binge in Leon's face. Leon gave him a bland smile in return.

"Yeah, I need to get on back anyhow." Turning to the pilot, Carl shook her hand. "Thanks, Jacqueline. You bringing next week's supplies, or is Kevin doing it?"

Jacqueline, that's right. Leon shook his head. He really was slipping, if he could get a name that wrong.

"Kevin. I'm taking a charter to Glacier Bay that day." Leaning sideways, Jacqueline waved at Leon. "Let me know if you change your mind about clubbing. Carl can call me on the radio."

Leon smiled and nodded. He let the smile fade when Jacqueline swung herself into the pilot's seat and Carl trotted back to the Jeep. Carl had the Jeep jostling back toward the forest by the time Leon heard the airplane's engine roar to life.

"It takes about ten minutes to get to the house," Carl said. "I'll lay down the ground rules as we go. If you have questions, ask 'em now. You might not see me again for a while."

"Busy groundskeeper, are you?" Leon gazed curiously around him as the Jeep entered the gap in the trees, plunging them into murky green gloom. Thick branches formed a deep emerald tunnel overhead. The chill breeze flowing through the open windows smelled of damp earth and evergreens.

Carl laughed. "The pilots really are local freelance pilots, not in the organization's pocket. Generates less gossip than if we hired our own. We keep up the myth of an eccentric multibillionaire living here to give the pilots and everyone else something harmless to say about the place, but you and I both know better."

"Yeah, I guess we do." Leon pulled his sunglasses off and stared at Carl's profile. "Don't they wonder why some rich guy lives out here on government land?"

"Of course they do. One of the rumors we've planted says the lake house owner gave millions of dollars and thousands of acres to help create Tongass National Forest, which of course makes this mythical owner out to be a benevolent and admirable soul." Carl shot a quick grin at Leon. "It keeps most people from trying to snoop, not that snooping here is any too easy. The forest is fucking near impenetrable in this area."

Leon wanted to ask why they'd built a secret government safe house in a national forest, but his gut told him to leave it alone. Some things, it was better not to know. "So. Ground rules."

"I know Jones told you no bar, but I know that look. If we don't wean you down, you'll be seeing spiders on the walls before the week's out." Carl shifted into low gear to climb a steep, muddy slope. The engine whined and the Jeep shimmied a bit, but stayed on the track. "The kitchen staff'll fix you Bloody Marys in the morning and wine in the evening, less each day until you're clean."

Leon grimaced. "Fucking hate Bloody Marys."

"Sorry, you didn't strike me as a Mimosa kind of guy." The Jeep topped the hill and rolled down the other side, picking up speed as it went. Carl shifted again, and the Jeep took the curve at the bottom on two wheels. "No straight liquor. No skipping meals. No raiding the pantry for flavoring extracts. Any and all alcoholic products will be kept under lock and key until you've got it out of your system. And before you go looking, we don't have any cold medicines or cough syrups, so make damn sure you don't get sick."

"Spoken like a man who's been in rehab before."

"Yep. Third time was the charm."

Studying Carl's craggy face, Leon could believe the man had seen the torturous drying-out process before. Probably prison as well. His eyes had that shuttered look all inmates got if they stayed in long enough. Leon knew he had that look in his own eyes. Jones had recruited him out of maximum security in New York at age twenty-one, with thirteen years of a fifteen-year grand larceny sentence left to serve. She liked to remind him of that when he started giving her attitude.

"Okay, meal times. Breakfast is at eight. Lunch at one. Dinner at six. Someone's in the kitchen at all hours in case you want a snack. You've got the run of the house, pretty much. Rule of thumb is, if it's not locked up, it's okay for you to play with it. If you come across a locked door, assume you're not supposed to be in there." Carl gave him a knowing sidelong look. "You'll surrender your lock-picking kit when we reach the house."

Fuck. "Aw, come on, you're taking away all my fun. Are the things behind the locked doors really that big a deal?"

The sudden ice in Carl's gaze answered Leon's question well enough. He decided to let it drop.

"There's a full gym on the first floor," Carl continued, shifting down again to cross a shallow stream. "There's also the biggest library you've ever seen in your life, and a media room with stereo, TV and Playstation. Oh, and we've recently had a laser tag range installed in the basement. Keeps your aim sharp."

Leon had his doubts about that, but kept them to himself. Shooting virtual enemies with lasers was a damn sight better than sitting on his ass watching TV. A real target range and his pistol would be better, but beggars can't be choosers.

"Jones mentioned a lake and trails," Leon prodded when Carl fell silent. For some reason, the idea of exploring the Great Outdoors was strangely appealing.

Guilt, you bastard. Ted loved hiking, but you always talked him out of it because you're such a fucking city boy. So now you think you're gonna make up for that by embracing Mother Nature. Fucking idiot.

"Oh yeah, you're really missing out if you don't spend some time exploring the property. The organization owns about a hundred acres, with trails all over. And the house sits right on one of the most beautiful lakes in the area, which is saying something." Carl grinned at him. "If you're thinking of running, don't. Once you leave this property, there's nothing but wilderness for hundreds of miles. People get lost out there from time to time. They hardly ever find the bodies."

"Duly noted." *Dammit.*

"I'm sure Jones told you we have a canoe as well. Don't try to go upstream in any of the rivers emptying into the lake, and don't go out at all unless it's nice weather. Otherwise, have at it and enjoy. The lake itself is safe enough, and there's little beaches here and there where you can put in and have a picnic or something."

A picnic. Leon snorted at the mental picture of himself lounging on a beach with a wicker basket full of sandwiches and fruit.

Carl kept talking, ignoring Leon's scornful interruption. "We'll expect you to be back by dark anytime you go out. Even if we weren't instructed to keep you here whether you like it or not, it's way too dangerous to be out after dark. The temperature can get below freezing even in the summer, and the bears are pretty bold."

Leon glanced out at the uninterrupted green wall rolling by outside as the Jeep bounced along. "What time does it get dark?"

"This time of year, not until almost ten o'clock. And the sun's up before five, so you've got plenty of daylight to work with." Carl glanced at him with a strangely solemn expression. "I know you probably didn't want to come here, Leon. No one ever does. But I can promise you won't feel hemmed in, or crowded. This is a great place to get your head together. Trust me on that."

Carl fell silent, staring out the window at the increasingly narrow and bumpy dirt track. Leon watched him from the corner of his eye. For the first time in months, he found himself wondering about another person's history. Had Carl once been in the same place Leon was now? Heart and soul ripped apart, mind and body careening down the slippery slope to self-destruction? Had he been saved by being dragged kicking and screaming to this place?

Leon ruthlessly squashed the bright flare of hope. Hope was for those too weak to see what was right in front of them. He'd never been weak.

After a few minutes, the dimness ahead began to lessen. The Jeep rounded a sharp curve, plunged down a short, steep slope and shot out into the open. Leon squeezed his eyes shut against the light.

Sliding his sunglasses into place, he cautiously opened his

eyes. And promptly forgot all about the lingering remains of his hangover.

"Fuck me," he breathed, almost to himself. "This place is fucking gorgeous."

Carl smiled, eyes shining. "Welcome to paradise, my friend."

Paradise was a good word for it. Ahead, the land sloped down toward a long, narrow lake of turquoise blue that glittered in the sunlight. Beside the lake sat a huge structure of roughhewn logs, its many windows reflecting the light. The vivid green grass rippled in the breeze, slapping against the sides of the Jeep as they made their way toward the house.

Twisting in his seat, Leon followed the faint tire tracks in the grass to where they disappeared into the deep, rather sinister darkness of the forest. The back of his neck prickled with a sudden sensation of being watched. If he squinted just right, he could almost imagine a pair of dark eyes staring at him from the shadows.

If anyone's watching you, it's probably the staff at the house, trying to get a look at the asshole they have to take care of for the next three months. Facing forward again, Leon kept his gaze firmly fixed on the house. He'd be damned if he'd let his imagination pick now to start running away with him.

"Well, here we are," Carl declared, pulling the Jeep up in front of the house and killing the engine. "Home sweet temporary home."

Leon opened his door, climbed out and dragged his duffle bag out of the back. He walked to the edge of the lake and stood there, gazing out over the sparkling blue water. On the other side, a forest so dark green it was nearly black climbed a steep slope to a craggy, white-capped peak. A waterfall tumbled over a series of rocks and off a short cliff into the lake, churning the gem-colored water into white foam. The sibilant music of it filled the otherwise unbroken quiet. The sunshine beat warm and soft on his brow, the slight breeze cool against his skin.

Leon drew a deep breath of clean, pine-scented air. The stillness soaked into him, bringing with it a wonderful sense of peace. He hadn't felt that way in almost a year. Not since the last time he'd lain in Ted's arms, their bodies wet with the sweat of lovemaking, Ted's kisses soft and sweet on his lips.

Ted would've loved this place.

To Leon's horror, tears pricked his eyelids. He hadn't cried when Ted died. Screamed and raged, yes. Threatened everyone and everything in his path, certainly. Hunted down and killed Ted's murderer, oh yes, couldn't forget that. He'd learned in the process how perilously close he was to becoming a monster like Frank Gold. But he'd never cried. Not once. To have it happen here and now, so far in time and space from the event which had sent his life spinning out of control, was puzzling and more than a little frightening.

Get a fucking grip, Fisher. He's gone, and all the tears in the world can't bring him back.

Gone. Ted was gone, forever, and there wasn't a damn thing Leon could do about it. He'd known that all along, of course, but for some reason his mind had chosen this July afternoon in this remote and beautiful spot to hammer that fact deep into his gut.

"Leon?" Carl called from somewhere behind him. "Let's get inside. You need to meet the rest of the staff, and I got things to do. You can come back out after you get settled."

"Yeah. Coming." Blinking behind his shades until the moisture in his eyes dried, Leon hoisted his bag more securely onto his shoulder and followed Carl into the house.

Chapter Three

To Leon's profound surprise, the forest fascinated him. He found himself standing at one or the other of the house's big picture windows at all hours of the day and night, mesmerized by the play of light and shadow beneath the trees. He fell into the habit of walking out to the end of the little pier at dusk, to watch night steal over the tree-clad slope across the lake. The sound of the waterfall in the dark soothed him. For the first time since Ted's death, he began to sleep through the night without waking.

After a couple of weeks, he started taking long walks in the meadow behind the house. Standing in the knee-high grass a few yards from the tree line, he often caught quick, furtive movements between the trees. Movements too careful and deliberate to be bears, or moose, or whatever the hell other animals roamed these woods. Many times, he had the distinct feeling he was being watched. Instinct told him whoever or whatever it was meant him no harm, but it made his skin prickle anyway.

Sometimes he felt as if he'd been plunked down in the midst of one of those fairy-tale forests full of talking wolves and child-eating witches. He had to laugh at himself when he realized how much the notion attracted him.

When he finally ventured more than a few yards into the woods, a month after he'd arrived at the lake house, he told himself it was just for exercise. A nice long hike every day, he rationalized, would go a long way toward getting his body back in shape. He'd lost his focus after killing Frank Gold, let himself go soft. Something about the clean Alaskan air made him long to feel strong and fit again.

He'd never acknowledge, even to himself, the part of him that just wanted to play in the woods, set out on adventures and uncover long-lost secrets.

"You have a radio, right? And a compass, in case you get lost?" Marie—the Head Babysitter, he called her, since he couldn't figure out what else she did—crossed her tan, muscular arms across her equally muscular chest and pursed her lips. She'd run into him just as he was leaving the house, and had decided she needed to know all about his plans. "I don't know, Leon. Maybe you should let me go with you."

Leon gritted his teeth and counted to ten in his head. "Marie," he said when he thought he could speak without being too insulting, "I'm not a fucking infant. I know how to follow a fucking trail."

"Yes, I know, but you've never been out there before and—"

"And Jones would have your hide if you lost me. I know, I know." Sighing, Leon ran his hand through his hair. His normal buzz cut had grown out enough for his natural curl to manifest itself. It bugged him, but the electric razor had proved inadequate for cutting it, and the assholes here wouldn't let him have anything sharp, God knew why. Even at his worst, he'd never been suicidal. "Listen, I swear I'll be a good boy and stay on the trails, okay?"

She still looked unconvinced. Glancing out the window beside her, she patted her neat blonde bob. "It looks like rain."

"Really? And here I thought I was wearing this as a fucking fashion statement." He gestured at the waterproof, fleece-lined jacket he wore. It had a warm, roomy hood, and he'd stuffed all-weather gloves into the pockets. "If I never go out in the rain, I'll never go out at all. There hasn't been a whole sunny day since my first week here."

She chewed her bottom lip, which usually meant she was about to cave. "You think you can be back by dinnertime?"

Fuck you. "Yes," he growled. "Now would you *please* get out of my way?"

Whether he'd actually convinced her of his ability to survive the trails on his own or she was afraid he was about to strangle her, he didn't know and didn't particularly care. She glared, but stepped away from the door she'd been blocking, which was all he wanted. He hefted the backpack he'd appropriated for this impromptu outing and strode out the door without looking back.

Outside, low-hanging gray clouds veiled the mountains. Gusts of cool wind brought with them the smell of impending rain. Leon drew the clean, fresh morning air deep into his lungs as he struck out toward the forest. He grinned up at the threatening sky. The storms here tended to be raw and savage, and he loved it. They made him feel more alive than he had in a long, long time.

"Not so long, really," he muttered into the rising wind. "Only a year. God, it seems like longer."

It seemed like forever, some days. He missed his old life. The thrill of the hunt, the pulse-pounding excitement of the kill. Going home to a man who knew what he was and loved him anyway. But that chapter of his life was over now, and it wasn't coming back. Though he hadn't admitted it to himself until recently, he'd known something fundamental in him had changed forever the moment he stared into Frank Gold's dead face.

He didn't regret killing Frank; regret was pointless, even if he'd been inclined toward it, which he wasn't. But Frank Gold was the first kill which left him feeling utterly empty. Like it hadn't even happened. That realization—not the killing itself, not even Ted's brutal death—had been the turning point for Leon, even if he hadn't known it at the time. A killer he'd been, and a killer he'd always remain deep inside, but he'd never again be the assassin he'd once been.

Not that he would ever tell Jones & Company that. He'd do his time here—which wasn't at all the unpleasant prospect he'd once thought it to be—convince Jones he'd straightened up, then skip the country the second her back was turned. He had connections Jones and her people knew nothing about. Leaving would be risky, of course, but what was life without a little risk?

Leon walked along the tree line for roughly a mile before striking uphill and into the woods. He'd seen a couple of other trails along the way, but this one held an appeal he couldn't quite define. Its narrow opening ducked under an arch of interlaced evergreen branches, the pine-needle paved floor rising steeply up the slope to wind away through the tree trunks. Something about it seemed mysterious and a bit sinister, and it drew Leon like a magnet.

On the trail, layer upon layer of green-clad branches offered shelter from the increasingly cold wind and the spatters of rain which had begun to fall. Leon trudged along, puffing from the exertion and cursing himself for allowing his body to become so deconditioned.

After a few minutes, the trail leveled off, and Leon was able to pay attention to things other than his overworked lungs. A riot of greenery grew in a wild tangle on the forest floor, creeping over the edge of the trail in places. The scents of a thousand growing things filled the air, underlaid with the aromas of rich earth and water. Overhead, rain pattered on the leaves and pine needles. Icy drops broke through to smack onto Leon's head and bare hands.

In the moist green twilight under the trees, Leon felt as though he were walking through a child's storybook. With no one there to scoff at him except himself, he decided to skip berating himself for his uncharacteristic excitement and just enjoy it. It had been far too long since he'd truly enjoyed anything.

Leon had been hiking for over an hour when he caught the faint sound of falling water from somewhere ahead. It grew louder as he went. Just as the ground began to tilt downward, the trail swerved to the right, uphill. He could just make out the spot where it curved back to the right again. Back the way he'd just come. Away from the water.

He stopped, cocked his head and listened hard. The deep roar told him it must be a large river, with some wicked rapids. Maybe even a waterfall. A much bigger one than the one across the lake from the house, if the sound was anything to go by.

He glanced back up the hill. He'd promised to stay on the trails and not wander off. But the boom of the unseen rapids drew him like gravity. He wanted to stand right beside the river, to feel the cold spray on his face, the earth vibrating from the force of the water thundering past. Was he really going to let a promise to some woman he didn't even like stop him?

"Fuck no," he growled. Finding a narrow ribbon of a trail branching off in the direction he wanted, he set off with a determined stride.

He had no idea what sort of animal had made the trail, but it was smooth and straight, and served his purpose well enough. Before long, the noise of the river was so loud the air shook with it. The path dipped downward, took a sharp turn to the left and ended abruptly on a large round boulder.

Leon stared, his mouth hanging open. Not five feet from the tips of his waterproof hiking boots, the river leapt down a series of steep rapids. The clouds had begun to break, letting random beams of sunshine through to catch on the foaming water. Raindrops sparkled on the trees and the tremendous ferns growing beside the river. The scene was so stunning, Leon couldn't even work up any disappointment that the threatening storm had never materialized.

A movement on the other side of the river drew Leon's attention. Stepping up to the very edge of the rock, he shaded his eyes with one hand and squinted into the shadows. The undergrowth in that spot was still now, but Leon could've sworn he'd seen it thrash a moment before, as if something large had brushed past it. Leaning forward as much as he dared, he tilted his head to get a better angle. He could almost see...

There. Eyes, staring straight into his. Big and dark and wary as a deer's, but definitely human.

Several breathless seconds passed while Leon and the person across the river stared at each other. Leon was torn between calling out to whoever it was, and hightailing it back to the house before the stranger found a way across the river. The person was an unknown, and therefore couldn't be safely ignored. Leon's gut told him the man—or woman? Leon couldn't be sure—was harmless, but he couldn't count on that. For all he knew, he was looking at someone as deadly as himself. If the person had a weapon and knew his way around the forest, things could go very badly indeed.

Stop being a pussy, Leon berated himself. *He already knows you're here. Find out who he is, and what he's doing here.*

His mind made up, Leon straightened, drew a deep breath, and cupped his hands around his mouth. Before he could make a sound, the bushes behind him rustled and snapped, and something huge and heavy slammed into him. He didn't even have time to be surprised before he fell face first into the river.

Chapter Four

The shock of icy cold knocked the breath out of him and made every muscle in his body go rigid. Summoning all the strength he could muster, he tried to push to the surface.

He couldn't move. No matter which way he twisted, he couldn't get his head above water. His face and hands had already gone numb with cold, his heart raced, and his lungs were beginning to burn.

Forcing himself to stay calm, he took deliberate stock of his situation. He was face down in the water and couldn't surface. Therefore, something must have him pinned. He had to figure out what part of him was pinned and get loose fast, or he'd drown out here.

For the first time, he noticed a fierce, sickening pain in his right calf. He knew that pain, having been stabbed once in prison. Something sharp was digging deep into the meat of his calf muscle. Several somethings, he thought, though his oxygen-starved brain couldn't be certain.

Whatever it was skewering his leg flexed and pulled. Cold water flowed into his sinuses as he was dragged halfway out of the water. Something that felt like massive ice picks raked the skin of his left shoulder blade, shredding his jacket like paper. Leon fought to free himself, grabbing at the river stones underneath him, but it was no use. His numb fingers wouldn't work.

Fuck, I'm gonna fucking drown in a river in Alaska. The thought was more irritating than frightening, and gave Leon a new burst of desperate strength. Gritting his teeth and ignoring the pain in his torn shoulder, he wrapped both forearms around a large, jagged rock protruding from the riverbed and pulled as hard as he could.

With shocking suddenness, the sharp things tore free of his leg, and just like that he was loose. His palms scraped along the rock as the vicious current ripped him away and into the thick of the rapids. The strap of his backpack caught on a dead branch stuck between two rocks. The pack hung there, slipping neatly free of the injured shoulder and nearly dislocating the other one as the current pulled Leon helplessly along.

Just as he was certain he was going to drown after all, his head broke the surface. He gulped air as fast as he could. More alert now, he struck out for the closest land, which was the opposite side of the river from where he'd been. He couldn't really see the bank, only tantalizing glimpses when the rapids flung him upward or sent him tumbling over a rock. But he could see the tops of the trees bobbing above the foaming water. He kept his gaze fixed as firmly on those green spikes as he could and forced his body to keep moving.

By the time the current tossed him into a relatively calm stretch at the bottom of the slope, Leon's arms and legs felt heavier than stone, and his entire body hurt. Black spots swam in his vision. He let himself drift into a scooped-out place in the riverbank. When he felt the river bottom scrape his back, he rolled over, dug his numb fingers into the silt and pulled until his head and shoulders were clear of the water.

Exhausted, he laid his cheek on the cold mud and shut his eyes. Logically, he knew it couldn't have been more than a couple of minutes since he'd stood on the rock beside the river, but he felt like he'd just completed a brutal triathlon. If he could rest here for a second, maybe he could gather the strength to get himself out of the river. The temperature had been almost fifty-five when he set out, warm enough that he should be able to avoid hypothermia and frostbite if he could get out of his wet clothes. Then he could see how badly he was injured, and try to figure out where he was.

One step at a time. First, he had to rest. Had to. Just for a minute. Only a minute...

℘

Leon opened his eyes, and was surprised to discover that he no longer lay half in and half out of the water. He'd somehow moved up under the trees, and was now curled under a crude shelter of lashed-together branches and green leaves. The river flowed a few yards away. His clothes—boots and socks included—had been removed, and a thick, coarse blanket tucked around him. A campfire ringed with river stones crackled nearby, giving off a wonderful warmth.

He pushed to a sitting position, hissing at the pain in his torn shoulder. A wave of dizziness hit him. His stomach rolled. He shut his eyes and waited for it to pass.

Opening his eyes again, he frowned at the makeshift shelter. He could buy that he'd dragged himself out of the water without remembering it. He could even believe he'd undressed in his semiconscious state. But there was no way he'd built himself a shelter and made a fire, and he sure as hell couldn't conjure blankets out of thin air. Which could only mean one thing.

Someone else had done all of that. And Leon was willing to

bet his left nut he knew who it was.

Keeping a sharp eye on the stretch of woods and riverbank visible from his shelter, he groped around him for anything which could be used as a weapon. All the available evidence indicated that his mysterious benefactor had his best interests at heart, but Leon wasn't taking any chances. His fingers closed over a broken stick with one end sheared into a point. He pulled it close to himself, holding it like he would a switchblade. It wasn't much, but it was better than nothing.

Feeling more secure now that he was armed—sort of—Leon leaned over to look out of the shelter. To the left, the rapids pounded in a constant roar, though they were far enough away that the sound was no longer deafening. To the right, the widening river flowed away through the forest. The land rose steeply on the far side, but the slope seemed gentler on the side Leon now occupied. Overhead, a single white cloud floated by. It seemed the weather had cleared, though the sharp, damp chill in the air spoke of more rain to come.

The sun had dipped low in the sky, meaning he must've been out for hours. Despite the stranger's apparent good intentions, it made Leon's skin crawl to know he'd been completely at the mercy of someone he knew nothing about.

Speaking of which, Leon saw no sign of his rescuer anywhere. Surely he didn't intend to leave Leon here alone, with night coming on?

And just when have you ever been afraid of being alone, jackass? Fucking deal with it.

Obviously, he couldn't get back to the house tonight, and he'd lost his radio and compass in the rapids. He'd have to spend the night here. A fire and shelter, he had. If he could locate his clothes, he could find some food. He could wait until first light, then set off for the house. The position of the setting sun told him the river flowed almost due west. All he had to do was follow it out of the forest, find a place to cross, and walk south along the tree line. Simple. They'd probably be looking for him, but he wasn't about to trust them to find him. Marie and her crew, Leon was convinced, couldn't find their collective ass with both hands.

Leon kicked off the blanket and bent his right leg up, trying to get a look at the damage. He wasn't surprised to see a bloodstained shirt wrapped around his calf, the sleeves tied in a tight knot to hold it on. The muscle throbbed with the slightest movement, but seemed to work okay. With any luck, it would hold his weight well enough for him to walk.

Clutching his stick, Leon crawled out from under the shelter. His body felt bruised all over, and his injured shoulder protested loudly. Gritting his teeth, he hauled himself to his feet.

He stepped gingerly on his right foot. Agony shot up his leg, hot and blinding. His foot came back up, he lost his balance and went tumbling to the ground.

"Fuck, fuck, fuck," he chanted, rocking in place with the force of the pain. "Jesus fucking *fuck*, god*damm*it!"

"The muscle's torn," said an unfamiliar voice. "You shouldn't try to walk on it yet."

Leon was up and turning toward the voice before he consciously realized it, his makeshift weapon held out in front of him. He dropped into a defensive stance out of habit, and promptly fell over again when his injured leg gave way.

Stop it. He's not your enemy. Yet. And you're in no position to be making enemies right now.

Forcing himself to remain still, Leon sat up and took a good look at the person who he assumed had rescued him from the river.

The man—more a boy, really—couldn't be more than eighteen, and wasn't anything close to the big, brawny specimen Leon had expected. He was tall, probably taller than Leon, but so thin it was amazing he'd been able to drag Leon from the water. He seemed to be all arms, legs and huge, wary brown eyes. A thick fur vest and a thermal shirt which had probably been white once upon a time hung from his shoulders. A chunk was missing from the bottom of the shirt, revealing a flat, pale belly bisected by a trail of dark hair. Battered jeans sagged on his thin hips and showed a fair bit of bony ankle between the frayed cuffs and the tops of his mud-caked boots. Tangled brown hair which looked like it had last been trimmed months ago with a dull knife fell in floppy chunks around a long oval face. He looked like some Hollywood director's idea of a crazed hillbilly.

Except he doesn't seem crazy. Leon studied the boy's big, long-lashed eyes and Cupid's bow mouth. *And he's awfully fucking pretty.*

Leon blinked, shocked at himself. He hadn't been remotely attracted to anyone since Ted. Why in the hell would he think this skinny, dirty kid was *pretty*? And since when did he go for the pretty boys, anyway?

"Who are you?" Leon demanded, trying with limited success to sound calm rather than threatening. "What happened to me?"

The boy's dark eyes narrowed, his gaze flitting between Leon's face and the sharp stick still clutched in his right hand. "My name's Grim. A bear attacked you. Pinned your leg with its claws. I shot it." He held up a large crossbow. "Didn't kill it, though. Just nicked its shoulder. But it ran away, so I guess that was good enough."

A crossbow. Fuck. Outgunned. Not that he'd expected

anything else. It wasn't too hard to beat a sharp stick as a weapon. "Why'd you shoot it?"

If Grim thought it an odd question, he didn't let on. He shrugged. "I didn't want it to kill you."

"Oh." Hardly the cleverest answer, but Leon found himself inexplicably tongue-tied. He'd never had a perfect stranger save his life before, especially for no particular reason, and he didn't know what to say.

Grim didn't seem to notice Leon's discomfort, though if the look in his eyes was anything to go by he'd certainly noticed Leon's nudity. "Go on and get back in the shelter. I brought food and water, and stuff to clean and bandage your wounds with. Other than my shirt, I mean."

The thought of Grim touching him made Leon's insides churn with a mix of apprehension and anticipation. Blaming his uncharacteristic level of emotional reaction on trauma and blood loss, Leon did as Grim said and crawled back under the shelter. Snagging the blanket, he wrapped it around his shoulders. The dropping temperature had him shivering, and his leg hurt with a ferocious, nauseating pain. Galling as it was, he needed the help Grim offered.

He still had the broken stick, in case he had to defend himself. Not that he thought he'd need to. If Grim wanted to kill him, he could've done it easily enough while Leon was unconscious.

Grim walked over, long legs covering the distance in a couple of strides. He crouched beside the fire, laid the crossbow on the ground—too far away for Leon to reach—and set down the ratty leather pack he'd been carrying. "What's your name?"

Leon thought about lying, but figured there was no point. "Leon. You said you have food?"

"Yeah. Some berries and dried meat, and fresh water. I

know it's not much, but that's about all I had ready to go." Unzipping his pack, Grim pulled out a clear plastic container with a red lid. He handed it to Leon. "Here. You can go on and eat while I get everything set up to clean your wounds."

Leon took the container, watching as Grim pulled a dented tin kettle out of his bag, filled it with river water and set it on the fire. "What, are we having tea too?"

"I'm boiling some water to clean your wounds with. I rinsed them out before, to get the worst of the dirt out, but you need boiled water and soap to get them really clean. You don't want those to get infected." Grim flashed a wide grin. "Don't worry, I'll let it cool first."

Smart-ass kid. Deciding that biting the boy's head off would be counterproductive at this point, Leon kept his retort to himself and opened the container. Several strips of dark, leathery meat lay on the bottom, covered by plump red berries. Leon had no idea what the meat or the fruit were, but the mix of sweet and spicy scents made his stomach rumble.

Scooping up a handful of berries, Leon crammed them into his mouth and bit down. The rich taste burst across his tongue, drawing a heartfelt moan from him. He snatched up a strip of meat and tore off a piece with his teeth, trying to ignore the intent way Grim was watching him.

"Do you want some?" Leon asked, hoping Grim would say no. He hadn't eaten since early that morning, and he was starving.

Grim shook his head. "I had some on the way back here." He fished an old-fashioned metal canteen out the pack and held it out to Leon. "Here. Water from my well."

Taking the canteen, Leon opened it and took a long swallow. The water was cold, crisp and delicious. He drank until the need for air stopped him, lowered the canteen and wiped his mouth with the back of his hand. "Thanks."

Grim settled cross-legged on the ground. Those huge eyes regarded Leon with solemn seriousness. "We can't stay here for long. They'll be looking for you."

The back of Leon's neck tingled. "Who?"

"The people at the lake house."

Leon stared at Grim, the food forgotten on his lap as he remembered all the times he'd stood just under the eaves of the forest and felt unseen eyes on him. "Have you been watching me, Grim? Huh?" The question came out sounding harsher than he'd intended, but he wasn't about to apologize. If the kid had been spying on him, he was going to be seriously pissed off.

To his surprise, Grim cringed away from him. The long legs bent up, thin fingers gripping his knees until his knuckles turned white. "I'm sorry. I didn't mean anything, I just... I just thought..." He bit his lip, his hair falling over his eyes and making him look about twelve in spite of his height. "I was just curious about you, that's all. I'm sorry."

Leon's instincts were screaming at him now, but not in the usual, prepare-for-attack way. Grim's hunched posture and downcast gaze gave Leon an ugly feeling in the pit of his stomach. He couldn't put his finger on it, but he knew he didn't like it.

"It's okay," Leon said, giving in to the sudden, inexplicable urge to soothe that frightened look from the boy's face. "You just surprised me, is all. I don't like people following me."

Grim didn't say anything, but his expression brightened and his lanky body uncurled, which Leon took as a good sign.

Leon popped another handful of berries into his mouth, shivering as a stray breeze found its way into his shelter. He wrapped the blanket tighter around himself. "I don't guess you brought me some clothes?"

"Yeah, I did. It gets too cold at night to be out here like...like that. Naked, I mean." Grim's eyes flicked downward, toward Leon's barely covered crotch. A faint blush colored the boy's cheeks before he looked away. "Your clothes were soaked. I took them back to my place to dry, all except your boots. You'll need those tomorrow, to hike up to my cabin."

Grim's gaze darted sideways, zeroing in on Leon's lower half once again. A picture flashed into Leon's mind—Grim flat on his back, naked, long legs wrapped around Leon's waist, head thrown back and mouth open as Leon pounded into him. It was vivid, unexpected and unwelcome. Shaken, Leon shoved the tantalizing vision away and forced his mind back to the situation at hand.

"What makes you think I'm going home with you?" Leon fished another strip of meat out of the container, watching Grim's face while trying to keep the turmoil inside him off of his own. "The people at the lake house will send someone after me. Maybe they already have. I was supposed to be back hours ago." He kept his lack of confidence in their actual ability to find him to himself.

Grim dipped his head so that his hair veiled his face. "I've watched the lake house for a long time. I've seen several people go there, but nobody ever leaves. They come out here like you did, and they just...don't come back."

Leon didn't answer. He kept eating, his expression carefully blank, as Grim rose, fished a large knife out of his pack and tromped off into the undergrowth behind the shelter. Several loud *thwacks* sounded. Probably Grim cutting more firewood, Leon figured.

He frowned at the stained blanket pooled in his lap. What Grim had just said bothered him, mostly because it rang true. Why the hell had Jones *really* sent him to Alaska? Was there something here he couldn't get back in L.A.?

Yeah, you could get dead. But if they planned to kill him, why not do it right away? What was the point in keeping him around for a fucking month first?

Because people get lost and die out here all the time. Because if you disappear, there won't be any questions for them to answer. Nobody'll know if a bullet got you instead of a bear, if your body's never found.

He didn't know if it was anything beyond wild speculation. But it fit what little he knew of the people he'd worked for over the past decade.

So go with the boy. If he turns out to be a psycho, take him down. If not, then you'll have a safe place to stay and recover, and think about things.

His mind made up, Leon went back to wolfing down the meat and berries. A couple of minutes later, Grim returned carrying two thick branches, sat on a rock by the fire and started hacking away at the wood. He didn't look at Leon, didn't speak, but the tension in his shoulders said he was acutely aware of Leon's presence.

Leon watched him from the corner of his eye. A thousand questions chased each other around his mind. Who was this oddly appealing boy with the even odder name? What was he doing out here in the wilds of Alaska, apparently by himself? And why was he so eager to help a perfect stranger? Leon wouldn't have done it.

Not everyone's an antisocial bastard like you, Leon reminded himself. *Maybe he's just one of those bleeding hearts who likes to help people. Like Ted.*

He didn't want to think about Ted. Not now. Thinking of Ted not only depressed him, it made him careless, and he couldn't afford to be careless right now.

Shoving all the memories and regrets to the dark corner of his mind where they'd lived for the past year, he finished his meal in silence. Grim was equally silent on his rock by the fire, intent on his work. Leon couldn't figure out what he was making, and Grim didn't seem inclined to tell him.

Grim looked up when Leon finished the food and set aside the empty container. "You done?"

Leon nodded. "Yeah. Uh, thanks. For the food and everything."

A wide smile lit up Grim's face, making him startlingly beautiful for a moment. Leon gulped. He wished his privates would stop taking such an interest in the kid. He didn't understand it, and therefore didn't like it.

"Spread that blanket out, and lie down on your stomach." Grim's gaze slid away from Leon's face and down to the ground, brushing between Leon's legs on the way. The blush rose in his cheeks again. "I'll get your wounds fixed up, then you can get dressed and go to sleep."

Leon managed to keep his crotch hidden while he maneuvered himself face down on the blanket. Having been injured more than once in the past, Leon knew exactly how much it hurt to have wounds like these cleaned and dressed without any drugs to dull the pain. His burgeoning erection would never survive it, which was just fine with him. He figured it wouldn't do either of them any good for Grim to see his cock at half-mast as it was right now.

The pain was even worse than Leon had feared. Whoever had taught Grim care of wounds in the field had not taught him to be gentle. Leon clenched his fists and bit his tongue and just barely managed to swallow the yelps and curses which wanted to come out.

By the time Grim taped down the loose end of the gauze

he'd wrapped around Leon's leg, Leon was covered from head to toe in cold sweat. He sat up, moving slowly. His leg and shoulder felt like they were on fire.

"I'm sorry," Grim said, his voice soft and uncertain. "I know I hurt you. I'm not very good at this, I guess."

Leon lifted a brow, surprised at the hint of fear in Grim's eyes. "You can't clean something like that without it hurting like fuck. I'm a big boy, I can take it."

Grim didn't answer, but his palpable relief was answer enough. Leon wanted to ask why Grim seemed alternately friendly toward him and afraid of him, but decided not to. It would probably scare the kid off, and Leon found himself very reluctant to have that happen.

Scrambling to his feet, Grim dug a gigantic blue hooded sweatshirt and a pair of thick camouflage pants out of his pack and handed them to Leon. "I hope these fit okay. They belonged to J..." He stopped, his expression going blank just a heartbeat too late to hide the brief flash of some emotion Leon couldn't quite identify. "I mean, they're just some old clothes I had laying around."

"They'll be fine." Leon took the clothes and managed what he hoped was a reassuring smile. "Thanks."

That sweet, lovely smile shone on Grim's face for a second before he returned to his rock by the fire. He sat with his back to Leon and picked up the pieces of wood he'd been working on before. Obviously, he was giving Leon privacy to get dressed. Leon appreciated the thought, even though his earlier problem was long gone.

He watched Grim's back as he dressed. Grim had shed the fur vest at some point, and Leon could see the curve of his spine where the stained shirt rode up to reveal the lower portion of his back. Leon had to fight the urge to lick the strip of pale skin.

Knowing he was attracted to this whip-thin, none-too-clean Grizzly Adams Junior did nothing at all to lift Leon's already glum mood. In all the time since Ted's death, Leon's sexual desires had lain dormant, and that suited him fine. He'd never looked forward to the inevitable return of his libido. Before Ted came along, he'd mostly gotten his needs met by high-priced call service men. The thought of going back to that was depressing, for reasons he didn't want to examine too closely.

The kid would probably go for it, Leon's sex-deprived body whispered. *I bet he's horny as fuck, out here all by himself for who knows how long. Did you see the way he was looking at you? Even if he's straight, he'd do you. You know he would.*

Grim raked his long, thin fingers through his hair in an ultimately futile attempt to keep it out of his face. He half turned toward Leon, shooting a tentative glance over his shoulder. The firelight gleamed on his skin. In that moment, he looked frighteningly young and vulnerable.

Leon smiled at him, an easy and natural smile like he hadn't used in months. It felt unfamiliar on his face, but it was worth it to see Grim's unease vanish and his smile return.

Rising to his feet, Grim turned around and held out the two pieces of wood, the shorter one now firmly lashed to the top of the longer one with thin, strong rope. "I made you a crutch. It's a long way to my place, and I think you shouldn't put much weight on your leg."

Leon took the crutch and examined it. Grim had cut the two pieces with astonishing speed and skill into a sort of tongue-and-groove assembly before tying them together. The top didn't budge when Leon tried to move it. It was crude but sturdy. Grim had even secured a thickly folded cloth to a stump sticking up at right angles to the main branch, so Leon could lean on it without hurting his hand.

Leon didn't even try to hide how impressed he was. "Damn, kid. Where'd you learn to do this sort of thing?"

Grim hunched his shoulders. "I had a sprained ankle about a year ago. I sort of worked out how to make a crutch then. I would've just brought my old one but I couldn't find it."

Leon gave his companion a sharp look. Grim seemed pleased that Leon found his handiwork acceptable, but the brown eyes were shuttered, the boy's expression careful. There was more to Grim's story than his unusual choice of where to live. Leon felt it in his bones, and it made him distinctly uneasy for reasons he couldn't pinpoint.

The upside was, Leon's undefinable discomfort made it much easier to ignore the physical attraction he felt for Grim. Which was good, because his gut told him that to give in to it could be very, very bad.

Setting the crutch on the ground, Leon made a show of yawning and rubbing his eyes. "I think I'll get some sleep. Thanks for the crutch, and...well, everything."

Grim nodded. "Sure. We'll start out at first light tomorrow. I can run to the cabin in about two hours, but it'll take you a lot longer, so I don't want to wait. Is that okay?"

"Yeah, no problem." Leon glanced around. "Where are you gonna sleep?"

"On the ground. I have another blanket. Don't worry, it won't rain tonight. Tomorrow, probably, but not tonight." Grim smiled, his right cheek dimpling just a little. "'Night, Leon."

"Yeah. Good night."

Rolling himself into his blanket, Leon settled onto his side and watched through half-closed eyelids as Grim pulled another blanket out of his pack. He wrapped the blanket around himself, curled up on the ground beside the fire and shut his eyes. Within seconds, his breathing slowed and the fingers clutching the edge of the blanket relaxed, and Leon knew he was asleep.

For his own part, Leon didn't feel the least bit sleepy, in spite of all he'd been through that day. Curiosity about Grim ate at him. He was dying to know more about the boy. Something about Grim made Leon want to protect him.

God, he looks so fucking sweet asleep like that. Makes me want...

Leon shook himself. The last thing he needed right now was to scare away the only person who could help him with unwanted advances. Or rather, advances Grim wasn't ready for, even if he did want them. Which, of course, Leon had no idea if he did or not.

The whole thing was confusing as hell, and turning it over endlessly in his mind was giving Leon a headache. Sighing, he clutched his broken stick to himself, shut his eyes and steeled himself for a sleepless night.

Chapter Five

Leon had expected the trip to Grim's cabin to be difficult. An injured leg plus God only knew how much rugged terrain to cross meant an arduous journey, no doubt about it. What he hadn't expected was how quickly it would sap his strength. Before their little camp was even half an hour behind them, Leon's heart was racing and his breath was coming short.

He gritted his teeth and soldiered on. No way was he asking Grim to let him rest. Grim would gladly stop, Leon was certain, and probably would think nothing of it. But Leon couldn't stand the thought of appearing weak in front of the kid. Stupid, maybe, but true.

Alpha posturing, his shrink would've called it, and spent several weeks in a pointless attempt to find the root of Leon's need to be macho. *Testosterone poisoning,* Jones would've said, and told him in her own cool and cultured way to get over it. Two completely opposite approaches, but both with the same goal—to make him fit to kill on demand again. Leon snorted, amused in spite of himself.

Grim glanced back from where he walked a few paces ahead. "Are you okay? Do you need to rest?"

"No," Leon lied, trying not to sound as winded as he felt. "Uh, how much further?"

"At this pace, probably another three and a half hours or so." Grim stopped, laying a hand on Leon's arm and forcing him to stop as well. He pinned Leon with a worried look. "Are you sure you don't want to stop for a while?"

"Yes, dammit, I'm sure." Leon grimaced when Grim flinched away from the growl in his voice. He was really going to have to learn to control his temper around Grim. "Sorry, I didn't mean to snap. My shoulder hurts like fuck, my leg hurts like five fucks, and yeah, I'm tired. But I don't want to stop. I just want to get where we're going."

"Okay." Grim chewed his bottom lip for a moment, concern clear as day in those big, pretty eyes. "Will...will you tell me? If you need to rest, I mean? I...I'm not trying to be bossy or anything, honest, I just... I'm just trying..."

"You're just trying to look out for me. Yeah, I know." Leon sighed, wishing he didn't get so exasperated with Grim's hesitant, almost submissive attitude. "Look, kid, I appreciate the concern, but I wish you'd just relax and stop fussing over me. I'm fine. And quit looking at me like I'm gonna hit you with my crutch, okay? I swear I won't hurt you. I'm a grumpy old bastard, that's all."

Grim's lips curved into a shy smile. "You're not old."

"I'm older than you by a long shot." Letting go of his crutch, Leon shook a developing cramp out of his hand before grasping the padded wood again. "What are you, eighteen? Nineteen?"

Grim shrugged as they started walking again, side by side this time as the rough trail widened a little. "Twenty, I think."

"You think? You mean you don't know?"

The guarded look came back into Grim's eyes. He stared straight ahead, not meeting Leon's gaze. "Yeah, I'm twenty. And I bet you're no more than five or six years older than me."

Leon had the distinct feeling Grim was lying. Not about his

age, but about knowing his age for certain. Deciding it didn't much matter either way, Leon elected not to say anything about it. "I'm thirty-one. *Way* older than you, kiddo."

Grim shot him a sly sidelong glance. "That's okay. I like older men."

Startled, Leon blinked over at Grim. Was he serious? Was he coming on to Leon?

Grim grinned, eyes twinkling, and Leon shook his head. "Smart-ass kid." He didn't know whether to feel relieved or disappointed. Surprisingly, he had absolutely no desire to rip the boy to shreds—physically or verbally—for playing with him like that.

They trudged on, climbing steadily uphill. Grim halted now and then to tell Leon the names of various trees or flowers, or to point out a particularly interesting variety of bird or insect. It was obvious he was doing it mostly to let Leon rest, but Leon didn't mind. The brief breaks were always just long enough for him to catch his breath, and for the cramp to ease from the hand clenched around the crutch.

If it hadn't been for the increasing pain and the bone-deep exhaustion, Leon would've enjoyed the hike quite a lot. The forest seemed determined to be as enchanting as possible. Everything was so green, Leon felt as if he were traveling through the inside of an emerald. Scattered beams of golden sunlight filtered through the branches to pick out a furled leaf, a small black beetle, the edge of a brilliantly colored flower. Overhead, birds chattered in the tremendous evergreens, and small animals scurried through the thigh-high ferns clustered between the thick tree trunks. The cool, humid air smelled of water and earth and a multitude of growing things.

Not for the first time, Leon thought this forest was easily the most beautiful place he'd ever seen. He wished he didn't feel three-quarters dead, so he could enjoy it more.

Eventually, the forest floor leveled off, then began tilting downhill. Leon found it far more difficult to maneuver down the slope than up. He kept expecting the crutch to slip in the damp earth and plant detritus and send him tumbling down the slope. Preventing that from happening took every bit of his energy.

Just when he was about to break down and ask if they couldn't camp another night, Grim stopped and laid a hand on Leon's shoulder. "We're here," he said, smiling.

Leon directed his gaze where Grim pointed. Through the wide trunks he glimpsed a cabin of gray, weathered wood nestled in a small clearing between the trees. Branches laced together over the peaked roof, covering the little building in a blanket of dappled sunlight and shade. Two small windows flanked a narrow doorway, which was reached by four wide, shallow steps.

At that point, the ramshackle cabin looked more inviting to Leon than any five-star resort on the planet.

"Come on," Grim said, giving Leon's arm a tug. "Let's get inside so you can rest."

"Amen to that."

From where they stood, the downward slope of the land eased into a blessedly level spot, then rose slightly before reaching the cabin's door. Leon made it across those endless yards of ground on willpower and determination, and stood at the bottom of the steps wondering if he had the energy left to climb them.

He started when he felt a hand on the small of his back. Turning, he saw Grim standing beside him, looking worried.

"Let me help you up the steps," Grim said, moving closer. "You're worn out, I can tell."

Leon wanted to refuse. But his legs were shaking, his grip on the crutch getting weaker by the second. If he didn't let Grim help him, he'd probably fall, which would be embarrassing as well as painful.

He scowled. "Yeah. Okay."

Grim slid his arm around Leon's waist. "Leave the crutch. You can lean on me instead. I'll come get the crutch once I get you inside."

Leon let the crutch fall to the ground and hooked his arm around Grim's shoulders. "All right. Let's do this."

The words sounded gruffer than Leon meant them to, but Grim didn't seem to notice. He pulled Leon tight against his side, and they took the steps together. Grim's grip was firm, holding Leon's weight with ease. The surprising strength in that slender body went straight to Leon's crotch, and he wished it wouldn't. He was too fucking tired to deal with it.

At the top of the steps, Grim swung the door open and led Leon inside. Light filtered through the windows in the front and a third window set in the opposite wall, lending the single spartan room a dim illumination.

Leon took a good look around. An ancient wood-burning stove nestled in the far right corner, a pile of neatly cut wood in a box nearby. In the opposite corner sat what looked like a futon in a homemade bedframe. A coarse blue blanket was spread over it and tucked under the edges. Between the bed and the stove sat a wooden hutch with built-in drawers. Pots, pans and mismatched dishes were stacked on the shelves. Beside it sat a large metal tub. A wide, deep dresser was pressed against the wall to Leon's left. Bits of white paint still clung to the battered wood. The bare wooden floor was clean-swept and adorned with a simple braided rug.

Not a weapon anywhere, except the crossbow, Leon

observed as Grim steered him toward the bed. *Maybe there's knives in one of the drawers.*

He'd pretty much dismissed Grim as a potential source of danger, but Marie and the lake house staff could still pose a threat. Plus he had no idea precisely where they were, or who else might frequent this forest. Being armed would go a long way toward making him feel safer.

"Lie down," Grim ordered, pulling back the blanket and threadbare sheet from the futon. "Are you hungry? I can fix you something to eat, if you want."

Leon shook his head as he sank down to the bed. "Not now. Thanks anyway." He lay back, wincing when the cuts in his shoulder pulled at him.

Kneeling on the floor, Grim started working open the laces of Leon's boots. "I know it was a rough trip. I'm sorry."

"Hell, kid, you saved my life, and you're still helping me. I'm not about to bitch about having to walk a while." Leon pushed up on the elbow of his uninjured arm. "You don't have to do that. I can take off my boots myself."

"I know. But I don't mind." Grim smiled, the dimple making a brief appearance in his cheek. "Relax. Let me take care of you."

Normally, Leon would've argued. He hated feeling helpless, and lounging on the bed while someone else removed his still-wet boots and filthy socks smacked of helplessness. But his body ached all over, his muscles felt weak and limp, and the deep gouges in his shoulder and leg hurt so badly he was afraid he might throw up. So he bit back his protests, lay down again and let Grim do what he wanted.

Grim had Leon's boots and socks off in a matter of seconds. Leon barely managed to avoid shouting in surprise when Grim lifted his bare right foot and dug both thumbs into the arch.

"Umm. Grim?"

"Hmm?" Grim didn't even glance up, keeping his concentration on what he was doing.

One knuckle massaged the tight spot in the ball of Leon's foot, and he swallowed a groan of pure pleasure. "What are you doing?"

"I figured your feet would be cramped up." Grim set Leon's right foot gently on the bed, picked up the left and began giving it the same treatment. He glanced up, catching Leon's eye. "I can give you an all-over massage, if you want."

Grim's dark eyes burned, destroying any hope Leon might've had that the boy hadn't meant it the way it sounded. Grim knew exactly what he was saying. Leon's mouth went dry.

"Uh...Grim..."

"Come on, Leon." The pad of Grim's thumb kneaded Leon's heel in tiny circles. "You're tired. You're hurting. And I'm here, and I want to help you." Setting Leon's foot on the bed, Grim moved to perch on the edge of the futon. He leaned over, staring straight into Leon's eyes. Leon could smell him, warm skin and stale sweat mingled with an unmistakable whiff of desire. "Let me help you, Leon. Let me make you feel good."

If Leon had entertained any doubt about how Grim intended to make him feel good, it was erased by the shock of Grim's hand on his crotch. The long fingers cupped Leon's balls through the fabric of his pants and gently squeezed. Leon couldn't keep himself from groaning out loud and pushing into Grim's caress.

"Grim, no. Don't." Leon grabbed Grim's wrist and pulled his hand away.

Above him, Grim went perfectly still, brown eyes wide and uncertain. "You want me. I know you do. I want to suck your cock, Leon. Why won't you let me?"

"Because... Because I..." Leon trailed off, shaking his head. He couldn't let Grim seduce him, no matter how much he might want it. Not when he was so dependent on the boy. "I'm tired, and I fucking hurt all over. I just don't feel like it."

Part of him wished he could take the kid up on his offer, but he knew he couldn't. Sex complicated things, and he didn't need any more complications in his life right now.

Grim stood, looking nervous. "Okay. Um...I'm sorry. I just didn't think. Sorry."

"It's okay. Maybe another time?"

The second the words were out, Leon mentally smacked himself. There wouldn't be any other time, and he knew it.

Oh, really? Come on, asshole, don't lie to yourself. You know damn well you'd have your dick down his throat by now if circumstances were different. How long do you think it'll be before you cave?

Leon suppressed a scowl. He hated it when his inner voice was right.

Strangely, Leon's promise of a future encounter didn't appear to placate Grim the way he'd hoped. Grim nodded and flashed a wide smile, but Leon thought he saw the swift gleam of apprehension in the boy's eyes.

The cold, ugly feeling from the previous day curled in Leon's stomach again. Grim's bold seduction combined with his almost subservient attitude—not to mention those brief, unsettling glimpses of fear in his eyes—spoke of something horribly unhealthy in the young man's past. Part of Leon was curious to find out what it was. The rest of him—by far the larger part—didn't want to know.

Crossing to the hutch, Grim opened the bottom cabinet and pulled out a towel, a washcloth and a rolled-up sleeping bag.

"What are you doing?" Leon asked.

"Getting out the sleeping bag for me, and washing supplies for you." Leaving the sleeping bag on the floor, Grim returned to the bed and stood gazing down at Leon. "I thought you might want to get washed up. Plus I'll need to clean your wounds again."

Leon groaned. "Can't we do that later? Right now I just want to rest."

"Okay. I'll bring you some water from the well and some berries, then I'm going fishing. Go on and sleep some, if you want."

The mere suggestion of sleep, coming on the heels of hours of strenuous hiking, was enough to make Leon yawn. He fought off the encroaching drowsiness. "Do you have a gun, or a knife? Any kind of weapon at all? Other than the crossbow."

"I have a butcher knife, and a hatchet." Grim ran a hand through his hair and shrugged. "But you won't need any weapon. I've lived here for about six years, nobody knows this place is here. You're safe."

Given the remoteness of the setting, Leon could easily believe that. But it didn't make him feel any more comfortable about being in here alone, injured and asleep. "Humor me. Give me the hatchet."

Grim hesitated for a second, biting his lip. Leon got the distinct feeling that the kid didn't want him armed. Which, of course, just made him want the weapon more.

After a long, silent moment, Grim fetched the hatchet from its spot behind the woodbox. Leon took it and inspected it. The handle was worn and cracked, most of the red paint rubbed away by years of use, but the blade was sharp and unrusted.

His gaze darting between Leon and the hatchet, Grim backed toward the door. "Okay. The stream where I'll be fishing isn't too far away, so if you need me just come to the door and yell. I'll hear you."

"All right." Leon settled the hatchet beside him on the bed, one hand clutched around the handle. "Thanks."

Grim nodded, turned and hurried out the door. It banged shut behind him. Leon shook his head. He wondered if he'd ever get used to Grim's odd and often contradictory reactions.

You have to live with him, at least long enough for these fucking wounds to heal. You'd damn well better learn to handle his weirdness. That kid's more than what he seems to be.

Leon had the feeling that underestimating Grim would be a huge mistake. He liked to think he didn't make those sorts of mistakes.

જી

His eyes had barely closed, it seemed, before he was woken by the pressure in his bladder. He looked around. Grim wasn't back yet, and he had no idea what time it was, or how long he'd slept.

Cursing himself for not having asked Grim where the bathroom was—if there even *was* one—Leon pushed to a sitting position and swung his legs over the edge of the bed. He sat there for a moment, examining how he felt. He could feel every single bruise on his body, and the places where the bear had clawed him throbbed and ached, but it was better than it had been before. If he could just get outside, he could limp behind a convenient tree to take a piss.

He managed to get his socks and boots on without too much difficulty. Glancing around, he saw the crutch Grim had made for him leaning against the wall at the foot of the bed. He stared at it for a moment, rubbing at the stubble on his chin. This whole situation was just too weird. He should, by rights, be dead. Not that he wanted to be dead. Especially now, when he finally seemed to be pulling himself together after all that had happened in the last year. But he knew without a doubt that he would have died if it hadn't been for Grim. There was no way Marie, Carl and the rest of the lake-house staff could have found him in time, even if they'd wanted to.

Even if they'd wanted to. Did they? Are they looking for me? And if they are, are they coming to help me, or to kill me?

With the more immediate issues of food, shelter and wound-tending addressed, Leon found himself questioning not only Jones' true motives in sending him to Alaska, but also Grim's assessment of the lake house. Just because the boy thought Leon's life was in danger from Marie and company didn't make it true.

"Why the fuck is he doing this anyway?" Leon wondered aloud, scratching his stomach under the sweatshirt. He could see—sort of—why Grim had shot at the bear, to keep it from killing him. That was a split-second decision. No time to think it over or to ponder the implications. Only time to act, or not, and Grim had chosen to act. It fit with what Leon had thus far gleaned about Grim's personality.

What he couldn't quite understand was why Grim had dragged him out of the river, built him a shelter and a fire, and hiked all this way to bring him food and dry clothes. It would've been so easy for him to just leave Leon there to die. In fact, now that he thought about it, Leon realized that Grim must have had to deliberately search the river for him in order to rescue him.

No matter how Leon looked at the question, turning it over and over in his mind, he couldn't understand why Grim would do such a thing. Nobody in their right mind would fault him for assuming Leon had drowned and leaving it at that. Maybe Grim was just one of those people who wouldn't be able to live with himself if he hadn't tried.

Or maybe your perceptions are just fucked up because you've killed so many people and haven't ever gone out of your way to save anyone. Maybe normal people do that sort of thing all the time.

Leon snorted. Of all the labels he could apply to Grim, "normal" was not one of them.

"Just fucking quit thinking about it," Leon ordered himself. "Go find a fucking bush or something, before he comes back and decides you need his help to piss."

The mental image of Grim holding Leon's cock while he peed was enough to galvanize him into action. Leaning over, he grasped the crutch, dragged it to him and planted the bottom on the floor. He levered himself to his feet, the hatchet firmly clutched in his left hand, cursing at the renewed agony in his leg when he tried to put weight on it.

It couldn't have been more than fifteen feet to the door, but fifteen feet had never seemed so far before. Gritting his teeth, Leon forced himself across the endless wooden expanse. When he reached the door, he rested his forehead against it and swallowed the nausea rising in his throat. He hated being this weak.

At the moment he reached for the door handle—awkwardly, because of the hatchet in his hand—the door swung inward. Leon stumbled back, pain licking flames up his leg. The hatchet clattered to the floor as his arms pinwheeled. Just as he lost his balance altogether and started to fall, an arm snaked around his waist, steadying him.

"God, I'm sorry," Grim exclaimed, his voice edged with

panic. "I was just coming in to get my knife for cleaning the fish, I didn't mean to knock you down. Are you all right?"

"Yeah, yeah, fine." Heart racing with the rush of adrenaline, Leon sagged against Grim's side. He hated himself for doing it, but he'd dropped his crutch and he was pretty sure his legs wouldn't hold him up right now. "I was trying to get outside. I really need to piss. Is there a bathroom, or do I use a tree or what?"

"There's an outhouse just behind the cabin. Do you want me to take you?"

Grim's body shook, and his voice had a distinct quaver. Frowning, Leon drew back enough to look into Grim's eyes. Grim's gaze skittered away, but not before Leon saw the pure terror underlying the boy's obvious relief.

"Why are you so scared of me?" Leon asked, searching Grim's face for answers. "I haven't done anything to you."

Grim tensed, his fingers digging into Leon's side. He kept his eyes downcast. "I'm not scared of you. I just... I knocked you over. You could've been hurt. That's all."

Leon stared at the young man holding him up. Moved by something he couldn't explain, Leon cupped one hand beneath Grim's chin to force him to meet his gaze. "I'm not going to hurt you, Grim. I promise. Okay?"

Grim nodded, brown eyes huge and intense. "Okay."

"Good. Now if you'll hand me that crutch, I'll just go to the outhouse. And no, I don't need any help."

To Leon's relief, Grim didn't argue. Waiting until Leon had steadied himself with a hand against the wall, Grim bent down and snatched the crutch from the floor where it had fallen. He handed it to Leon without a word.

"Thanks," Leon said, tucking the crutch under his arm.

"Uh, how do I get to the outhouse?"

"Go around to the right toward the back of the cabin. You'll see it." Grim licked his lips, fingers twisting together. "Call if you need me. I'll be out front cleaning the fish."

"Sure."

Leon stood there for a heartbeat longer, wanting to remove the glaze of fear from Grim's eyes but not knowing how. For the first time in his life, he wished he had the same talent with words that he had with weapons. At that moment, he wanted nothing more than to make Grim smile.

Listen to yourself, you asshole. Turning soft over some weird, skinny kid just because he wants to suck your dick. Just keep it in your pants. You don't fuck him, he can't fuck with your head.

Thus decided, Leon turned away. He could feel Grim's gaze like a brand between his shoulder blades. Hating the way Grim's scrutiny made his skin blaze, he wrenched the door open and stumbled down the steps.

Chapter Six

In the beginning, it hadn't been too difficult for Leon to keep his promise to himself to stay out of Grim's pants. For the first couple of days, he'd been so tired that even a trip to the outhouse completely sapped his strength. Pain had also done its part to keep any sexual urges at bay. It thumped through his leg and shoulder in hot waves, day and night without respite, killing every desire other than to be free of it.

On the morning of the third day, Grim left before dawn and came back deep into the night with a plastic sandwich bag full of prescription painkillers. Leon hadn't asked where he'd gotten them, just like he hadn't asked where Grim had acquired his stash of rice, dried beans and dressing supplies. Grim clearly didn't have the money to purchase any of it. Some things, Leon figured, it was better not to know.

The drugs dulled the pain enough to make walking to the outhouse or sponging the grime and sweat off his body bearable. Oddly enough, he had no qualms about indulging in narcotic-induced relaxation in Grim's presence. He felt safe with Grim. Not safe enough to drop his guard completely, but safe enough to let himself get the sleep his body needed.

About a week after coming to the cabin, Leon's pain started to lessen as the wounds began healing. He tapered off the pills, taking them only at night so he could sleep. The rest and the tender care Grim gave him did him good. His energy started to return, and along with it came a renewed surge of lust for the young man tending him.

He blamed Grim. In all that endless, torturous time, Grim didn't touch him at all, except to clean and re-dress his wounds every day. Leon would've believed Grim's offer to suck him off had been nothing but some kind of waking dream brought on by blood loss, if it hadn't been for the heat in Grim's eyes whenever he looked at Leon.

As it was, fantasies of what might have happened if he hadn't turned Grim down were driving Leon slowly insane. Every time he closed his eyes, he pictured Grim's sweet, pretty lips wrapped around his cock. It didn't help that Grim was always stretching so that his shirt rode up to show his belly, or bending over to pick something up off the floor and thus giving Leon a good look at the curves of his spine and his firm rear end. Once when Leon went out to use the outhouse, he was treated to the sight of Grim with his shirt off, wiry muscles bunching as he chopped firewood. It had taken every ounce of Leon's stubborn determination to keep limping toward the outhouse instead of tackling Grim to the ground and having him.

The day his weakening determination disintegrated for good, Leon returned from a short walk in the woods to find Grim standing completely naked in the big metal tub, dripping wet and streaked with soap. Leon leaned on his crutch in the doorway of the cabin and watched Grim bathe. The boy was utterly shameless, standing there with his bare skin glowing in a beam of sunlight as he scrubbed his shoulders with a threadbare washcloth. Water and suds sluiced down his back and over his taut little ass, and ran in rivulets through the sparse growth of dark hair on his legs. Strong, streamlined muscles shifted under his pale skin as he moved the cloth down to wash his belly.

The whole thing was clearly calculated to force Leon's hand. To break down the last of his resistance to Grim's subtle but persistent seduction and turn their strange relationship into a more physical one.

The fact that it was working galled Leon beyond belief.

Leon was halfway to the tub before he realized he'd decided to take what Grim so transparently offered. Grim gave no indication of knowing Leon was there, but there was no way he didn't hear the thump-and-drag of Leon's painfully slow, crutch-assisted gait. He knew Leon was there. He could probably smell Leon's lust. Leon could sure as hell smell Grim's. The sharp, wild tang of male arousal filled Leon's nostrils, overwhelming the scents of water and soap as he closed the distance between them and laid his left palm on the hollow of Grim's hip.

Grim dropped the washcloth when Leon's fingers moved to cup one firm butt cheek. "Leon..."

"You're a tease," Leon murmured, thumb dipping into the crack of Grim's ass. He felt sweat prickle between his shoulder blades. Grim had evidently stoked the fire in the woodstove, and the room was bordering on tropical. "You've been teasing me for days."

"I'm not teasing." Moaning, Grim slid his feet further apart, opening his thighs for Leon's wandering hand. "You know I want you. You said maybe another time. Is this another time?"

"Maybe it is." Snaking his left arm around Grim's waist, Leon pulled him close. Grim's skin was warm and wet, and smelled of homemade soap. "What do you want, kid?" Leon nuzzled the damp hair at the nape of Grim's neck. "You still want to suck me off? Or maybe you want me to fuck you?"

A tremor ran through Grim's body. "I...I w-want whatever

you want. Anything."

Something in Grim's voice seemed off. But his words had Leon's prick hard as stone and tenting the fabric of his pants.

He slid his palm down to cup Grim's balls. The skin there was smooth and silky, downed with fine, surprisingly soft hair.

Leon traced his fingers up Grim's rigid shaft, finding foreskin drawn back from a wide, leaking head. He growled and pressed his groin against Grim's backside. "You got rubbers?"

Grim arched into Leon's touch. "Oh…no, I… No. I don't."

Swearing under his breath, Leon rested his forehead against Grim's neck. He felt like he'd die if he didn't get his cock inside Grim's sweet little ass right *now*.

You're clean. He's lived here in the middle of fucking nowhere for six years, so he probably hasn't had many partners. Either way, you're topping. Acceptable risk. Do it.

His mind made up, Leon traced his fingers down Grim's chest and pinched one pink nipple, making him squeal. "Let's move this party to the bed."

Grim stepped out of the tub and wound a damp, slippery arm around Leon's waist. He smiled, dark eyes gleaming. "Lean on me. I'll help you."

Leon did, wondering when he'd become such a pansy. Not only was he having to be helped to bed like a sick old man, but his heart was hammering like a fucking virgin bride's, and it wasn't from exertion, or even anticipation of his first sexual encounter in more than a year. The sight of Grim's radiant smile—not his wet, naked body, but his fucking *smile*—made Leon's insides lurch and his skin tingle, and that made him nervous as hell.

Lust, he could handle. But this didn't feel like a nice, simple case of wanting a good fuck. It felt like something more.

Maybe a "friends with benefits" type of thing. Except they weren't friends. Leon didn't have *friends*. Plenty of victims, numerous casual lovers and the soul mate he'd lost, but no friends. Even if he did, he and Grim hadn't had any real opportunity to *become* friends.

Don't think about it. Not right now*, for fuck's sake.*

When they reached the bed, Grim lowered Leon gently to the mattress and sat beside him, pressed close to his side. The scent of Grim's skin, clean but underlaid with the musky spice of desire, sent a wash of pure need through Leon's body.

He reached between Grim's thighs and gave his balls a light squeeze, making him gasp. "You'd better have lube."

"Yeah." Leaning over, Grim reached under the bedframe and emerged with a half-empty bottle of liquid lubricant in his hand. He gazed at Leon through a veil of dark hair. "How do you want me, Leon? Anything you want. Any way you want it. I'm all yours."

Leon slid his palm up Grim's shaft, thumb gently working his foreskin. "You on all fours, me behind you. Easier for us both, I guess."

Grim's cheeks flushed. Setting the lube beside Leon and scooting backward on the bed, he rose to his hand and knees, planted his elbows on the futon and arched his ass into the air.

He turned to stare at Leon over his shoulder. A drop of water ran down his cheek and onto his lip. He licked it off, swiping his tongue into the corner of his mouth and wedging it there for a moment. He didn't say a word, but the fire in his eyes spoke volumes.

"Fuck." Leon pulled his sweatshirt off and threw it on the floor, then began the process of getting out of his pants without standing up. He couldn't stop staring at the little dark pink hole between Grim's pale buttocks. Maybe it was just because he hadn't had sex in so long, but he'd never seen anything more inviting in his life.

His pants were puddled at his ankles when he realized he'd forgotten to remove his boots. Cursing under his breath, he worked the laces loose, yanked off his boots and kicked off the pants. His injured shoulder twinged, but the pain wasn't nearly as bad as it had been in the first few days. Certainly not bad enough to keep him from fucking Grim like he'd wanted to do since the first time he saw him. At least the kneeling position would keep his leg from hurting too badly.

Free of his clothes, Leon levered himself onto his knees and moved behind Grim, the lube clutched in one hand. Giving in to a sudden urge, he bent and licked between Grim's shoulder blades. His skin tasted clean and sweet, tinged with a slight bitterness from the remains of soap.

"Leon," Grim moaned, pushing his rear against Leon's groin. "Fuck me. Please."

The husky plea sent what little blood remained in Leon's brain racing for his crotch. Straightening up, he opened the lube and poured a generous amount into his hand, then dropped the bottle onto the futon. He slicked lube over Grim's hole and slipped one finger inside.

"Oh!" Grim glanced over his shoulder, his gaze not quite meeting Leon's. "What...? What are you...?"

Oh fuck. No. No way. He pulled his finger out of Grim's ass. "Should've told me this was your first time, kid," he growled, hearing the barely contained irritation in his voice but unable to help it. He didn't trust himself to be gentle right now, yet he didn't want to be rough with a boy who'd never had sex before. Especially Grim.

Grim shook his head. "No. It's just... There's only been one, and he...he never did anything like that before he fucked me."

A vague uneasiness fluttered in Leon's belly. He ignored it. He could ponder the mystery of Grim's past—and the apparently rather brutal bastard who'd taken the kid's virginity—later. Right now, he was dying to come. And after what Grim had just said, he was determined to make it the best fuck of Grim's life.

Resting his left hand on the small of Grim's back, Leon massaged Grim's hole with his right thumb. "I'm just getting you ready. You need to be stretched out some, so it won't hurt when I fuck you." He pressed his index finger inside. The ring of muscle clamped down hard. "Whoever you were with before, he should've done this too."

Grim hummed when Leon added a second finger. "That feels good."

"Yeah." Leon twisted his fingers, sliding them deeper to search for Grim's gland. Finding the little firm spot, Leon rubbed it.

Grim let out a soft gasp. His thighs spread further, his chest lowering to rest against the futon. "God. Please, Leon, please, fuck me."

How could any man resist the raw lust in Grim's voice? Leon sure as hell couldn't. Tugging his fingers free of Grim's ass, he took his cock in his hand and rested the head against Grim's loosened hole. A bit of steady pressure, and the tip of his prick popped inside.

Grim's ass rippled around him, hot and silky and wonderful. Leon stilled, panting. Resisting the urge to thrust was the most difficult thing he'd ever done, but he managed. He refused to be like the asshole who'd introduced Grim to sex. Being a professional killer didn't mean he had to be an inconsiderate lover.

Grim mewled, fingers digging into the blanket. "Leon.

Please. Oh, please."

With a huge effort, Leon forced himself to pay attention to the signals from Grim's body. He heard desperation in Grim's voice, but no hint of discomfort. A tiny, experimental thrust told him Grim's hole had relaxed enough for his cock to slide easily in and out.

The way Grim groaned and pressed back against him obliterated the last of Leon's hesitation. Clamping his hands onto Grim's hipbones, Leon shoved his prick in to the hilt.

He tried to keep his movements slow and controlled, his rhythm steady. But it had been ages since he'd been with anyone, and Grim was so warm inside, the grip of his ass so snug and satin soft, Leon couldn't fight it. Within minutes, he was pounding into Grim as hard as he could, sweat dripping into his eyes and Grim's sharp cries echoing in his ears.

When the orgasm began to build inside him, Leon started to pull out. *He* knew he was clean, but Grim didn't, and Leon figured he wouldn't want a rectum full of spunk unless he knew it was safe. Grim reached back and grabbed Leon's hip, keeping him from moving.

"Don't," Grim rasped, shooting Leon a wild stare over his shoulder. "Come inside me."

The words alone were enough to send Leon beyond the point of no return. He threw his head back and let out a hoarse shout as he filled Grim's ass with his semen. His eyes squeezed shut, his body trembling in the throes of his release. God, it had been so fucking *long* since he'd felt this. He wanted to draw out the moment forever.

All the strength ran out of his limbs along with the last pulse of come from his cock. He pulled out and collapsed onto the mattress beside Grim, panting like he'd just sprinted a mile.

Grim sat up on his knees and shoved his hair out of his

eyes, a soft smile curving his mouth. "Did you like fucking me, Leon?"

Leon laughed. "You could say that, yeah."

"Good."

To Leon's surprise, Grim crawled to the edge of the bed, hopped to his feet and sauntered back to the tub. A thick white stream oozed down the inside of one thigh as he stepped over the edge of the tub into the water. His cock, Leon couldn't help noticing, was soft. The lack of a wet spot on the bed told Leon the boy hadn't come, so he must have lost his erection during sex.

Grim didn't seem at all bothered by it. In fact, he looked blissfully content. He hummed a low, minor key tune as he swabbed the semen off his ass and legs.

Leon tried to tell himself he wasn't disappointed that he hadn't made Grim come, but it didn't work. He had to admit he'd looked forward to Grim's orgasm almost as much as his own. It was puzzling—and confidence shattering—that Grim not only hadn't come, but seemed perfectly happy about it.

Grim's humming faltered. Leon looked up at him, and frowned. Grim stood facing Leon, washing himself just like before, but something was different. His body looked stiff, his shoulders tense. A faint tremor in his hands sent a shower of droplets raining from the washcloth he held.

He's scared again, Leon realized, watching Grim bend to wash his legs. *What the fuck?*

Ignoring the twinge of pain in his shoulder, Leon sat on the edge of the bed and leaned his elbows on his knees. "Grim, why are you acting like you're scared of me again? I promised not to hurt you. I keep my promises."

Grim's gaze met Leon's for just a heartbeat before darting away. "I know. I'm sorry. You...you were scowling. I thought I'd made you mad. I was gonna ask if you needed anything else, honest, I just wanted to clean up first."

"Anything else"? Fuck, does he mean what I think he means?

Staring at Grim's carefully blank face, Leon had no idea how to answer. Even though Grim hadn't said so, he obviously didn't believe Leon wouldn't hurt him. Maybe he believed Leon didn't *intend* any harm toward him, but his fear of Leon's anger hadn't abated one bit. Worse, Leon got the feeling Grim saw himself not only as Leon's caretaker, but also his sexual servant.

Leon knew that idea hadn't come from him. Looking back, he could see the pattern in Grim's behavior from the start. Which meant that at some point in Grim's past, some sick fucker had indoctrinated him with these twisted ideas about himself, and his place in a relationship.

The possibilities were numerous. But Leon thought he knew who'd done it. Anyone selfish enough to make a virgin boy think sex had to hurt was probably capable of some pretty unsavory things.

You should talk, Leon's long-disused conscience prodded, sitting up and shaking the dust off itself. *How many people have you murdered? How many times have you stared at some kid no older than this one, scared shitless just like Grim is right now, and pulled the trigger?*

Leon shoved the needling voice to the back of his mind. This was different. It had to be.

Grabbing his crutch, Leon struggled to his feet and hobbled over to Grim. The boy just stood there, blinking at the soapy water swirling around his feet. Fine tremors ran through his body.

"Grim, look at me," Leon ordered.

Grim raised his face, his gaze locking with Leon's. His pupils were huge, his breathing rapid and erratic, but he didn't move, didn't look away.

That takes fucking balls, to stand there and face someone who you expect to do fuck-knows-what to you any second.

Admiration for this strange, beautiful boy swelled in Leon's chest. Flustered by the unwanted feelings and having no clue how to handle it, Leon ended up speaking more gruffly than he'd intended. "Look, I think your asshole boyfriend did some pretty shitty things to you before, but he's not here anymore. I'm here now, and I'm not like him. I'm not going to hurt you, and I sure as hell don't want you to be my sex slave. If we fuck, it has to be because we both want to, not because you think you have to do whatever I want. Or whatever your misguided little brain *thinks* I want. Got that?"

Grim's expression didn't change, but his trembling subsided. "You don't want me, then?"

"I thought it was obvious I *do* want you, seeing as how I just had my cock up your ass. What I *don't* want is a submissive. Too damn complicated." Sighing, Leon rubbed his free hand across his forehead. "You can trust me, Grim. I swear."

For a moment, Grim just stared at him. He stared back, willing Grim to believe him.

When Grim finally nodded and smiled, Leon knew it wasn't completely real, but he also knew it was all he was going to get. For now, anyway.

"I'm going back to bed," Leon said, turning and clumping across the floor to the bed. He eased himself down with a grimace. His wounds ached after the recent exertion. "You wore me out."

"Okay." Stepping out of the tub, Grim snatched a ragged

81

blue-and-white striped towel off the floor where he'd left it and started drying off. "Do you need a pain pill?"

"No thanks." Leon lay back, too tired to even bother with his clothes. It was warm enough to sleep naked. He watched Grim walk over to the dresser and pull on a pair of worn jeans and a blood-red sweater. The way his pale skin peeked through the partially unraveled shoulder seam made Leon want to drag him back to bed again. "You going someplace?"

"Hunting." Grim sat on the end of the bed and pulled on a pair of stained socks. The big toe of his right foot poked through one of the larger holes. He reached for his battered leather hiking shoes and shoved his feet into them. "I want a rabbit for a stew tonight."

"You can shoot rabbits with a crossbow?"

"Yeah." Grim shook the hair out of his eyes and turned to look at Leon. "I don't know about anyone else, but *I* can. I'm really good."

Grim's wide, confident smile put that cute little dimple in his cheek, and Leon felt a sudden urge to kiss him. It was rather alarming, considering he hadn't kissed anyone since Ted. Hadn't met anyone he'd *wanted* to kiss.

Until now. Until Grim, with his soft pale skin and incomprehensible ways, and the sweet-but-sly smile which always made Leon's heart race. Leon itched to pull Grim close and open that tasty mouth with his tongue.

Don't. Just fucking don't. Don't complicate things now. Keep It Simple, Stupid. Kissing takes it too fucking far. K-I-S-S, but don't kiss.

If Leon was the type of person who giggled, he would've done it. Clearly, the unaccustomed exercise had made him too tired to think straight. Yawning, he lay down and pulled the blanket up over himself.

Grim stood and smiled down at him. "Go to sleep, Leon. I'll be back in a couple of hours."

Leon nodded, eyes already closing. Too late, he remembered his groin was sticky with dried semen and lube. *Fuck it. I'll wash later.*

In the twilight between waking and sleeping, Leon could've sworn he felt the touch of soft lips on his brow. *Just your imagination, asshole,* he told himself, and drifted into a deep sleep.

Chapter Seven

"Steady," Grim whispered, his breath warm on Leon's ear. "Take the time to get your aim right, then squeeze the trigger with a slow, continuous pressure."

"I'll lose him," Leon murmured, staring at the sleek young buck through the scope of Grim's crossbow. "Animals are...easily startled. Right?"

Grim chuckled, and Leon let out a silent sigh of relief. He'd almost said "animals are harder to kill than people," and had bitten his tongue at the last second. After nearly six weeks, Grim still didn't know what Leon did—or rather, *had* done—for a living, and Leon saw no good reason to change that.

"We're upwind of him. He can't smell us, and it seems like he can't hear us either. If he did, he'd have bolted by now." Pressing his body against Leon's back, Grim made a minute adjustment to Leon's grip, then released him and stepped back. "You won't get a better shot than this. Go for it."

Leon drew a deep breath and let it out, feeling his tension run out along with it. A familiar, icy calm flowed into him—the centered emptiness of the mindset into which he'd always fallen during a hit.

Focusing on the animal currently drinking from the river, he squeezed the crossbow's trigger the way Grim had taught him, increasing the pressure of his finger until the arrow sang through the air and hit its target with a muffled thump.

The deer let out a strange, rusty noise and tossed his head so hard one of his antlers smacked into a low-hanging branch. He began loping away from the water, but only got a few paces before he staggered and fell. He lay still, the arrow protruding from his throat.

Shaking a stray lock of his ever-lengthening curls from his eyes, Leon raised his eyebrows at Grim. "How's that?"

Grim's wide grin threatened to split his face in half. "That was fantastic. Are you sure you've never used a crossbow before?"

"Never. I've used a rifle, though. It's different, but similar enough to feel kind of familiar." Leon glanced sidelong at Grim as they tramped through the underbrush to the spot where the deer lay. The breeze blew his hair over his eyes again, and he shoved it impatiently away. "I've seen you shoot this thing, Grim. You're pretty damn impressive with it. Where'd you learn?"

"The man I used to be involved with hunted with a crossbow. I watched him a lot, and I taught myself whenever he…" Grim shot a shuttered look at Leon, "…whenever he let me handle it."

Leon watched Grim squat beside the felled buck and cut the arrow loose with his knife. In the weeks they'd spent together, the only thing Leon had learned about Grim's previous partner was that Grim didn't like talking about him. Sure, he'd drop tidbits of information, such as the bit just now about the crossbow hunting. But on the few occasions when Leon had asked more direct questions, Grim had clammed up and refused to say a word.

Not that he'd ever told Leon in so many words that the subject was taboo. He'd never once said, "Sorry but I don't want to talk about him." Instead, he would develop a sudden need to pick berries, or catch a fish for dinner, or cut more firewood.

Every time Grim changed the subject, or scurried out of the room as if running away from the questions, Leon's curiosity about the whole thing cranked up a notch. He had no idea *why* finding out more about Grim's mysterious former lover was so important to him, but it was. He suspected the nameless man was behind the majority of Grim's strange behavior, from his subservient attitude during sex to the way he still flinched whenever Leon showed the least suggestion of anger.

It was frustrating as hell, wanting so badly to know and not being able to find out. Leon would've been seriously tempted to tie Grim to a tree and wring it out of him, if he hadn't known how much it would traumatize the kid. Leon had become extremely fond of Grim, to the point where the thought of anything hurting him in any way made Leon feel cold and sick.

He didn't like to consider what *that* meant.

Grim set his knife and the arrow on the ground. "Let's gut this guy and get him back to the cabin. The meat would be better if we drained the blood and let it hang for a few days, but the weather's been too warm for that lately. Don't want it to go rotten." He grinned. "Venison steaks for dinner tonight, and enough jerky to last for ages."

Leon's stomach rumbled at the mention of food. It had become almost a Pavlovian response in the past few weeks. Grim hadn't exactly starved him, but Leon never got quite his fill either.

Between the relative scarcity of food and the hard daily work of his newly primitive life, he'd lost weight and gained muscle tone. He hadn't looked—or felt—this good in years. Still, he missed the ready availability of food in his former life. He had occasional vivid dreams of hamburgers, chips and beer.

Strangely—or not, now that he thought about it—good food was about the only thing he missed. Maybe that was why he hadn't yet made any attempt to leave. He'd placed the blame for his continued presence here firmly on his injuries, but maybe there was more to it than the slight limp he still sported. Maybe he simply didn't want to leave this place. He'd grown used to the cool green quiet of the forest, and the unpressured routine of his days. The fact that he had to work for everything here— hauling water from the well, hunting and fishing, cutting firewood—gave him a satisfaction he never thought he'd find in such a simple life. He had no desire to go back to what he'd been before.

Or maybe you just don't want to leave Grim.

Now *that* was dangerous territory. He and Grim had grown closer over the past weeks, drawn together by shared pleasures, not all of which were sexual. Grim's rescue and seduction of Leon had started it, but the moments that entrenched Grim deep under Leon's skin were the little ones. The way Grim hummed ballads and lullabies as he worked, sometimes singing lilting folk songs in his surprisingly rich voice. The discovery of an old chess set, teaching Grim to play, and the delighted smile on Grim's face the first time he beat Leon at a game. The look in Grim's eyes whenever he stalked Leon across the bed—wild, feral and hungry.

The things he'd begun to feel for Grim had veered into some dark, murky waters, and he didn't want to examine them too closely.

Shaking off his pensive mood, Leon walked over to Grim. "Okay, how do we do this?"

"I'll gut the carcass. You can take my hatchet and dig a hole to bury the intestines and stuff in." Rummaging in his backpack, he pulled out the hatchet and a small lump of cloth-wrapped homemade soap. He set the soap on the ground, well away from the dead deer, and handed the hatchet to Leon. "If you don't mind, that is."

"Of course I don't mind. How many times have I told you, I want to start doing more of the work around here?" Leon frowned at the deer. It was small for a buck, but it looked heavy. "How do we get it back to the cabin?"

"I'll carry it." Grim grinned, evidently reading Leon's skepticism in his face. "It's easier than you'd think, and the cabin's not far."

Leon watched Grim dig the knife into the deer's abdomen and start sawing it open. His stomach churned in spite of himself when a mass of grayish, blood-smeared intestines spilled onto the ground. If it bothered Grim at all, Leon couldn't see it. His admiration for Grim, already considerable, went up.

Hatchet in hand, Leon squatted beside Grim and started hacking a rough hole in the ground. "I could carry it," he offered.

Grim shook his head. "I'm used to carrying my kills, it's not a big deal. You're here to help me get it onto my shoulders, that's more help than I usually have." Grasping the edge of the slit he'd made in the deer's belly, Grim stretched it open with one hand and started cutting the animal's insides loose. The nauseating stench of perforated bowels wafted through the air. "Besides, I'd be afraid it might leak on those cuts in your shoulder."

"They're healed." Leon switched the hatchet to his left hand and gave it an experimental swing. The wounds pulled sharply at the surrounding skin when the hatchet thunked into the ground. "Well, mostly healed. And we have the tarp, so the fluids shouldn't get on me anyway." Leon gestured at Grim's backpack, in which he'd stashed a battered old tarp before they'd set out that morning.

"I know, but there's still a couple of spots on your shoulder that aren't completely scarred over yet. And you know the tarp has holes in it. It'll keep the mess down, but it'll still be messy carrying it." Sitting back on his heels, Grim shook his hair out of his eyes and pinned Leon with a solemn look. "I know you want to help. Believe me, there's plenty to do aside from carrying the carcass back. But I'd never forgive myself if you got an infection from this deer." He dropped his gaze to the ground. "Don't be mad."

"I'm not mad." Leon sighed, wishing he didn't feel so clumsy and useless most of the time. Grim had been incredibly patient with his efforts to learn everything from starting a fire to identifying edible fruits and fungi, but Leon had no patience at all with himself. He hated not knowing how to do what he needed to do. "Okay, you carry. But you have to let me help you butcher it."

Grim's smile lit up the dim forest. "Deal."

They worked in silence for a while, Grim hollowing out the deer's abdominal cavity while Leon dug a pit sufficient for burying the animal's viscera. Together, they scooped the guts into the hole and filled it in. Leon tamped down the loose dirt with the flat of the hatchet.

"We can wash in the river," Grim said, rising to his feet with his usual fluid grace.

"Grim, you read my mind." Leon wrinkled his nose at his hands, coated in blood and worse. He'd killed a lot of people, but he'd never had to butcher anyone, thank God. It made him feel defiled in a way a nice, clean hit never had. "Please tell me we're not going to have to hunt very often. This is an awful damn lot of really disgusting work."

Grim laughed. "Yeah, I guess it is. Don't worry, we should

only have to hunt every couple of months. Less, when the salmon are running."

"Good." Leon smiled. It seemed that Grim planned on keeping him around for a while. Warmth welled up inside him at the thought.

Snatching the soap off the ground, Leon followed Grim down the steep bank to the river's edge. Leon scrubbed his hands and forearms clean while Grim used moss from the bank to scour the knife, arrow and hatchet. Once all the gore was gone from his skin, Leon handed the soap to Grim. He stood beside the water and watched Grim lather up. The way Grim slid the misshapen lump between his hands was downright obscene.

Leon had to laugh at himself. He'd never wanted to be a piece of soap before.

"What?" Grim glanced up, one corner of his mouth hitching up. "What's so funny?"

"Me." Leon nodded at the suds oozing from Grim's fist. "I was just thinking how much I'd like to be that soap right now."

Grim gave him a sultry look which was wildly out of place with his grubby clothes and dirt-smeared face but nevertheless made Leon's heart thump. Picking up the scrap of cloth, Grim wrapped the soap in it and set it on the ground, then rinsed the lather off his hand. Rising to his knees, he leaned forward and nuzzled Leon's crotch.

Leon bit back a moan as Grim mouthed his swelling prick through the fabric of his pants. He rested his hands on Grim's head, petting the thick, silky hair. "Thought you wanted to get the deer back to the cabin."

"It can wait a few minutes." Grim stared up at Leon, brown eyes blazing. "I want to suck you. Can I?"

Desire jolted through Leon's blood. He licked his lips.

"Yeah. Okay."

Beaming, Grim flipped open the button of Leon's pants and pulled the zipper down. A sharp yank on the waistband of the pants sent them puddling around Leon's ankles. Grim wrapped his fingers around Leon's shaft and ran the tip of his tongue delicately around the underside of the flared head.

"Christ, kid," Leon panted, fingers digging into Grim's hair.

Grim licked a wet stripe up the length of Leon's shaft. "Will you say it, Leon? Please?"

Leon swallowed a couple of times, trying to find his voice. Grim's predilection for being ordered to perform various sex acts made him uncomfortable, but he couldn't deny how much it turned him on. It helped that Grim's eyes had mostly lost the near-terror which used to lurk beneath the lust when they fucked.

Leon preferred not to think about why Grim wanted to be ordered to do the things Leon knew he wanted to do anyway, or why his gut insisted that something other than a sexual kink was behind it. He thought he could guess. Questioning Grim's motives might drive him away, and that was the last thing Leon wanted, for lots of reasons.

"Suck my cock, boy," Leon demanded, in the commanding tone he knew Grim liked best. "Right now."

A visible shudder ran down Grim's back. With a swift, smoldering glance at Leon's face, Grim opened his mouth and slid Leon's cock deep into his throat.

Leon let out a hoarse groan. He held onto Grim's hair for dear life as the world spun around him. Grim had sucked him off nearly every day since the first time they'd fucked, but Leon had yet to tire of it. The kid was incredibly talented. He sucked cock like a pro, but with far more enthusiasm than the typical hooker. Whenever he wrapped those luscious lips around

Leon's prick, Leon had trouble remembering his own name.

As usual, Grim had Leon on the brink of release within a few minutes. The first time Grim sucked him, Leon had blamed his shooting so fast on the fact that he hadn't had his prick in a man's mouth in over a year. When it continued to happen time and time again, he'd had to admit that the combination of Grim's skill and his obvious enthusiasm for giving head was simply greater than Leon's staying power.

Leon grunted, knees shaking when Grim deep-throated him. "Fuck. Close."

Humming happily, Grim slid his mouth from the root of Leon's cock to the tip. The head popped free of his lips, and he dipped his tongue into the slit before looking up at Leon. "Leon? Which?"

He knew what Grim was asking—did he want to come in Grim's mouth, or on his face? They'd played this game disturbingly often in the past weeks. Leon nearly sobbed in frustration. Thinking straight was almost impossible at this point. He wished Grim would just do whatever *he* felt like doing, instead of wanting Leon to instruct him every step of the way.

"Your mouth," Leon gasped, forming the words with a huge effort. "Swallow it."

Grim actually laughed before leaning in to apply a brain-scrambling suction to Leon's prick. Leon, torn between irritation and the melting warmth he felt in the pit of his stomach whenever Grim laughed like that, decided neither emotion could compare to the sensations exploding from his groin. He came with an echoing shout. The rhythmic contractions of Grim's throat as he swallowed sent hot bolts shooting through Leon's insides.

He stood there swaying slightly, blinking at the trees while Grim licked the few stray drops of semen from his genitals and tucked him carefully back into his pants. Fabric moved against his skin as his zipper was tugged up and his pants buttoned.

When Grim stood, Leon grabbed his wrist. "I want to suck you too."

Grim went pale. "Why?"

"What do you mean, 'why'? You suck me off all the time. You seem to like it pretty well. Didn't it ever occur to you that I might like sucking cock too?"

They stared at each other. Grim looked stunned, as if this had indeed never occurred to him. He hadn't let Leon touch his cock since their first time together, not even to jerk him off while Leon was fucking him. Not that he expressly forbade it. In fact, he'd never said no to anything Leon wanted. He'd simply squirm out of reach, or start touching himself whenever he felt Leon's hand between his legs. It was nothing overt, but enough to let Leon know that sort of touch wasn't welcome. He didn't understand it, but he couldn't complain, seeing as how Grim seemed to have an endless appetite for his cock.

At least Grim stayed hard lately during sex. Sometimes he even came with Leon's prick buried deep inside him, whimpering and shaking as he spilled on the sheets. While those moments soothed Leon's bruised ego, the one-sidedness of their physical relationship was starting to feel increasingly uncomfortable. Grim had never even slept in the bed with him, insisting on spending his nights in the sleeping bag on the floor. Leon was determined to get them on more equal footing, no matter what it took.

Not that sucking Grim off would exactly be a hardship. The sight of Grim's uncut prick never failed to make Leon's mouth water, and he was dying to taste.

"Do you really want to suck me?" Grim asked, his voice soft and tremulous.

"Yeah, I do." Sinking to his knees beside Grim, Leon slid a hand onto his thigh. "Why does that surprise you so much?"

Grim stared at the ground. Leon could see the pulse pounding in his throat. "I...I don't... John, he never..."

He trailed off, but Leon got the point. "You mean that fucking selfish bastard never once sucked your cock?"

"He wasn't selfish!" Grim snapped, eyes blazing. "He saved me! He took care of me! Don't you ever talk about him like that again."

Leon blinked, shocked into silence. Grim had never once raised his voice to Leon, never shown the slightest sign of bad temper, and Leon had no idea how to react. It surprised him that he felt no anger toward Grim, but he didn't. All he felt was the same peculiar squeeze in his chest which he got every time Grim revealed a glimpse of his closely guarded past.

"How long were you with him?" Leon asked, keeping his voice low and calm. "I get the feeling you were together for a while. It just surprises me that he never gave you head. Seems wrong to me."

Grim hunched over, his hair falling forward to hide his face. "It doesn't matter, he just...he didn't like to do that."

Leon couldn't help noticing that Grim hadn't answered the question of how long he'd been with his previous partner, but he didn't push the issue. Grim was twitchy enough already, and Leon didn't want to scare him off completely.

At least he now had a name to put with the shadowy figure in his head. John. He wondered where this John person was now, and what he was doing. *Probably being a selfish fucking bastard with some other kid who doesn't know any better,* he thought with a grimace.

Stifling a sigh, Leon shoved the hated blond curls out of his eyes. "Okay. So. You ready to get this deer back to the cabin?"

He ached with the need to taste Grim's come, but he knew now wasn't the time to force the issue.

Not that he was giving up. Not by a long shot. There would be other opportunities.

Gathering the knife, arrow, hatchet and soap, Grim rose to his feet and went to squat beside the deer's carcass. His gaze still wouldn't meet Leon's. "Yeah, I guess we should start on back. Skinning and butchering this guy is gonna take some time." He returned the arrow to the quiver, sheathed the knife and shoved the soap into the backpack.

Nodding, Leon crouched on the other side of the buck. Grim was reaching into the backpack for the tarp, when something rustled in the undergrowth several yards behind them. To Leon, it sounded exactly like every other noise made by one of the many animals inhabiting the forest. Grim, however, froze in place, eyes wide and head cocked to listen.

"What—?" was as far as Leon got. He snapped his mouth shut when Grim held up a hand to silence him. He gave Grim a questioning look.

Grim shook his head. Snatching up his crossbow and backpack, he rose into a half-crouch and ran silently toward the river, motioning Leon to follow. He headed for a spot a few feet downstream where the riverbank rose in a mossy, fern-clad hummock.

Calling on the skills he was half-afraid he'd lost, Leon mimicked Grim's hunched posture and hurried in his wake. The faint sound of his footfalls was muffled by the thick carpet of plant detritus underfoot and the late September wind tossing the branches overhead.

Just ahead, Grim turned a sharp corner dangerously close to the river and disappeared. For a heart-stopping second, Leon couldn't figure out where he'd gone. Then he saw the opening yawning in the bank and realized what had happened. He shoved aside the trailing vines which nearly obscured the cave's mouth and ducked inside.

The space in which he found himself wasn't so much a cave as a hole in the ground. It was barely large enough for him to kneel beside Grim. The chatter of the nearby river and the smell of wet earth filled the tiny space. Roots dug into Leon's knees and dangled from the low ceiling to brush his hair.

The light leaking through the vines edged Grim's face in gold. The tight, wary set to his features reminded Leon of the first time he'd seen him, staring across the river just before the bear attacked. Leaning close, Leon put his mouth next to Grim's ear.

"What the fuck's going on?" he murmured. "Why are we hiding?"

Grim turned and tilted his head to whisper in Leon's ear. His hair brushed Leon's cheek as he moved, and Leon shivered. "Someone's out there," Grim said, his voice barely more than a breath.

Leon didn't ask how Grim knew it was a person rather than an animal. Hunting with Grim in the time since his leg had healed enough to walk long distances, he'd learned not to question the boy's instincts.

It could be Jones & Company, riding to the rescue six weeks late, he mused, staring at the rotting tree stump just outside their hiding place. Of course that wasn't necessarily a good thing. Grim had never wavered in his belief that the staff of the lake house would kill Leon if they found him, and Leon couldn't altogether discount that. Especially since it made such a convenient cover for the wave of near-panic he felt at the thought of leaving Grim behind.

The minutes crawled by. A dull ache began in Leon's

injured leg, growing worse with every second. He was on the verge of asking Grim if it was safe to leave, when the thump of heavy boots sounded overhead.

Leon went still. He and Grim glanced at each other. To Leon's surprise, Grim pressed himself close to Leon's side, his arm snaking around Leon's waist. It seemed perfectly natural for Leon to put his arm around Grim's shoulders in a protective embrace. Grim tensed for a second, then relaxed against him. Leon had to admit it felt good, in spite of the circumstances.

Muffled voices filtered down from overhead. As the footsteps came closer, Leon could just make out what the two people—a man and a woman, it sounded like—were saying.

"I know I heard something," the man said, sounding defensive. "Somebody shouted."

"It was probably a moose or something, dumbass." The female voice was bored, as if she had to put up with wild goose chases from her partner all the time. "There's nobody here, and it doesn't look like anybody's been here either."

"What about the deer?"

"What about it? Deer don't die in the woods?"

"It was shot." Impatience tinged the man's voice.

The woman snorted. "That looks like a claw mark in its neck. It was probably a bear attack. We probably scared it off."

"God, Wallins, how stupid are you?" The man's impatience came through loud and clear. "This damn thing's been gutted, nice and clean. Bears don't do that. People do."

"Bears gut their prey all the time. It's probably already eaten the guts."

"Listen, if it was a bear—"

"Shut up, Jenson. Just shut the fuck up."

Wallins' voice was flat and emotionless, and Leon's blood

ran cold. He recognized that tone, having heard it in his own voice whenever he'd been required to deliver a message to a target before killing them. Wallins was clearly the more dangerous of the two, and Leon was grateful that she evidently didn't know much about bear kills versus human kills.

Jenson was silent for a moment. When he spoke again, he sounded nervous. "Wallins, come on, you know as well as I do this deer wasn't killed by a bear. It was shot, probably by an arrow, then gutted in preparation to butcher it for food."

"What if it was? Do you see any people around? 'Cause I sure as hell don't."

"They must've left."

"Without their kill? Come on, Jenson."

"Well..." Jenson didn't seem to have an answer for that. Leon shook his head, amused in spite of himself that neither of the unseen people had even considered that the buck's killers might be hiding nearby.

"Yeah, that's what I thought." There was a moment of quiet. Leon held his breath, wondering if the two had left. Then Wallins spoke again. "Look, we can report it as a possible poaching, I guess. But I still think it was a bear."

"Fine. Whatever. Let's head out, we're gonna be late getting back to the station as it is."

"Go on ahead, I'll meet you in the clearing in a minute."

Neither Jenson nor Wallins said anything else. Leon expected to hear footsteps tromping away from the river, but there was nothing. He got the distinct feeling that the man and woman—park rangers, maybe?—were fighting a silent battle of wills, and he couldn't help wondering why.

After a moment, a heavy tread sounded, moving away. Soon it was lost in the rush of the river. Glancing sideways into

Grim's eyes, Leon read his own thoughts reflected there—
Wallins was still up on the riverbank. Watching, waiting.

Leon held perfectly still, in spite of the pain now screaming
in his leg. Grim pressed closer, his fingers digging into Leon's
ribs. He wedged a knee underneath Leon's buttocks. The shift
in position allowed Leon to let Grim's leg take some of his
weight. It was such a relief Leon had to swallow a sigh. He gave
Grim's shoulder a gentle squeeze by way of thanks.

It seemed like ages before they heard the faint thud of
footfalls again. They waited until the sound died away and the
songs of birds and insects rose again before emerging from the
little cave. Grim crawled out first, taking the crossbow and
backpack with him, then reached a hand back in to help Leon
clamber onto the riverbank.

Leon hissed as the blood rushed back into his feet and pain
thumped through his leg. "What the fuck was *that* all about?"

Frowning, Grim shook his head. "I don't know. I'm pretty
sure they were park rangers, but the woman acted weird."

"Weird how?" Leon asked, though he agreed. He was
curious to know what Grim thought about it. Especially since
he didn't seem especially surprised by the whole episode.

"Weird, because there's no way a park ranger would
actually think that deer had been killed by a bear." Grim
scratched at an insect bite on his neck, staring into the middle
distance. "She knew her partner was right, but she didn't want
to say so. She wanted him to drop it."

"And, she wanted him to go away so she could have a few
minutes alone here," Leon mused. He leaned against a gnarled
tree root protruding from the hump of moist earth behind him.
"I don't know much about park rangers, but that does seem
pretty strange."

Grim didn't answer. He seemed as puzzled by the incident

as Leon was, but something in his face set Leon's instincts clamoring. An expression hinting that he'd made a connection Leon lacked the information to make. What that connection was, exactly, Leon had no idea. But a familiar fear shone in Grim's wide eyes, and it gave Leon a cold feeling in the pit of his stomach.

"Well," Leon spoke up after a long silence. "They're gone now, so let's get our dinner and get the fuck out of here before they come back."

Clutching his crossbow in a death grip, Grim brushed the fingers of his free hand across Leon's wrist. Leon recognized it as the invitation it was. He took Grim's hand, and they climbed the bank together.

The buck still lay where they'd left it. As they approached, Leon saw something white lying beneath one limp foreleg. A piece of paper. "Looks like Ranger Wallins left us a little something."

All the color drained from Grim's face. "What? Why would she do that?"

Leon frowned. Something was off. Grim was far more upset than a note from a forest ranger seemed to warrant. "Probably just warning us about poaching," he said, managing to keep his deepening suspicion out of his voice. "Like you said, she's bound to know a bear didn't kill this deer. I guess she just wanted to give us the chance to stop poaching in the national forest without turning us in."

Grim bit his lip. He wanted to believe what Leon had just said; it was written all over his face. Letting go of Leon's hand, he bent and picked up the note. "Yeah, that's what it is. It says to stop shooting deer."

Over the last few weeks, Leon had learned what a good liar Grim was. He constantly hid his true thoughts and feelings, and he lied about inconsequential things all the time. Leon had no idea *why*, but he accepted it as simply part of Grim's strange personality. As far as he knew, Grim hadn't been dishonest about anything that mattered.

Until now. Whatever was on that paper, Leon was sure it wasn't a warning about poaching deer. And he was equally sure it was important.

"Let me see it," Leon said. He held his hand out.

Grim laughed, the sound loud and fake. "Why? I just told you what it said."

Apprehension coiled in Leon's gut, though he wasn't sure why. "Grim. Give me the note."

The demand was cold and menacing. Grim cringed, and Leon hated himself, but he didn't back down. Every instinct he had told him he *had* to read that note. That it was the key to so much of what had been puzzling him, the answer to so many of his questions. About Grim, about John and the cabin, about his own safety in the outside world. So he kept his hand out and held Grim's gaze.

It took longer than he thought it would, but eventually Grim hung his head and laid the note in Leon's palm. He stood still and quiet, his hair hanging over his face, while Leon scanned the words scribbled in blue ink on the paper.

The note was short, but bits and pieces of the past six weeks clicked into place as Leon read.

John, I know this buck is your work. You haven't come for supplies in a long time, though I noticed you took the drugs I left you a few weeks ago. I can't get any more, so don't ask. If you turn me in, I swear to God I'll tell every paper in this country about that boy in Portland AND the one I know you're keeping now. Don't think I won't. If I go down, I'm taking you with me.

Leon's mind raced as a partial picture of the situation

coalesced in his head. Wallins must've been involved in something illegal. John had known it, and had struck a deal with her—food, shelter and secrecy in exchange for his silence about whatever she was involved in. If that was the case, John must have felt he had something to lose if Wallins turned him in.

A boy in Portland. And now, Grim. Leon's stomach churned.

Leon crumpled the paper. "What the fuck?" he growled, aiming a penetrating glare at Grim. "Did you know about this? Did you know what he was doing?"

He wished he didn't sound so furious, but he couldn't help it. Grim wasn't even the target of his anger. John was. John, who'd taken Grim's virginity with no consideration for his pleasure or comfort, who'd made him think he wasn't even *worth* consideration, who Leon suspected had brought Grim here in the first place, six years ago.

God, he was only fourteen.

Grim's gaze met Leon's for a split second before darting away again. "I...I d-don't..."

Behind the glaze of terror in Grim's eyes, Leon saw a thread of mingled curiosity and shame, and revelation blossomed in his head.

He held out the note to Grim. "Read it."

Grim scraped his thumbnail up and down the stock of his crossbow. His eyes wouldn't meet Leon's. "I already did."

"No. You didn't." Stuffing the paper in his pants pocket, Leon went to Grim and grasped his shoulders. "You can't read, can you?"

Squeezing his eyes shut, Grim shook his head. His cheeks flamed red.

A giant fist seemed to constrict around Leon's chest. He

didn't know if the faceless bastard John was behind Grim's lack of education too, but it wouldn't surprise him.

Wrapping his arms around Grim's waist, Leon pulled him close and tugged his face down to kiss his forehead. He wished he could tell Grim it was okay, that it didn't matter to Leon that he was illiterate, but he'd never been good at talking, and the words wouldn't come.

I have to find out more about John, Leon decided, pressing his cheek to Grim's and running both hands up under his sweater to caress his back. *I have to find out who he was, and exactly what he did to make Grim this way.*

The hell of it was, Leon was sure he already knew, and it made him burn with impotent fury at the sick fuck who'd turned Grim into the wounded person he was now.

When they drew apart, Grim's eyes were suspiciously red. He gave Leon a wan smile, the smile Leon had come to associate with Grim feeling melancholy and not wanting to show it. "It's got to be nearly noon. Let's start back now."

Grim turned away before Leon could answer. Leon waited until they'd wrapped the dead deer in the tarp and hefted it onto Grim's shoulders before he spoke again.

"I want you to tell me about John," Leon said, sounding more abrupt than he'd wanted to. "That's not an order or anything. I'd just like to know, is all."

Grim's knuckles went white where he grasped the buck's leg. "I will. But not yet." He glanced at Leon, his expression anxious. "Is that all right?"

No, it's not fucking all right. I want you to tell me what he did to you. I need *to know, once and for all, if I'm right.* "Yeah. That's all right."

The relief radiating from Grim's face was worth the frustration of being put off yet again. Leon hid his anger at

John behind a smile, and he and Grim struck out for home in a rather strained silence.

As they made their way through the pathless forest, a hard knot formed in Leon's belly. Change was coming. He could feel it, and he dreaded it. Dreaded having his suspicions about Grim's past confirmed. Dreaded what might be in store for both of their futures. Dreaded the destruction of something which had, in a few short weeks, become as necessary to him as food, water and air.

For the first time, Leon realized exactly how much he'd come to depend on Grim. Not on the food and shelter Grim provided, but on Grim himself. His smile, his laughter, the way he stuck his tongue out when he was concentrating really hard, the little kittenish sounds he made when Leon fucked him. His presence had become woven into the fabric of Leon's days, and he didn't want to give it up.

Watching Grim trudge through the trees, shoulders slumped under the weight of the buck, Leon could finally admit to himself what it all meant. Acknowledging what he felt was a relief, in a way, but it was also a burden.

Loving Ted had been easy. Loving Grim, however, was going to be downright daunting.

Leon didn't realize he'd fallen behind until Grim stopped and twisted around to look at him. "Leon? Is your leg okay?"

"It's fine," Leon said, and forced a smile. "I was just thinking."

Grim's expression clouded, as if he were afraid of what Leon might be thinking, but he didn't say anything. He turned and started walking again. Leon followed, wondering what the coming days would bring. Wondering if the unexpected happiness he'd found was about to be destroyed, either by his own out-of-control emotions or by a crooked ranger with an ax to grind.

I won't let that happen, Leon swore to himself, watching the play of sunlight and shadows on Grim's back. *I won't let anything take this away from me.*

"Snow's coming soon," Grim said, squinting at the sky as they passed through a small clearing. "Another couple of weeks, at most. We'll need to start putting up dried meat and fruit for the winter."

"And cutting firewood," Leon added. He smiled at Grim, and Grim smiled in return.

Leon lifted his face to catch the freshening breeze. The late September air smelled of the approaching winter. With any luck, Wallins would stay away, Jones would give Leon up for dead, and by the time the land thawed again in spring Leon and Grim could go about their lives without the threat of the outside world hanging over them.

Leon had always believed hope was for weaklings. For people too blind or stupid to see life for the dark, cruel thing it was. So what did that make him now?

Shaking his head, Leon tamped down his whirling thoughts and forced himself to focus on the here and now. He and Grim had an afternoon of hard work ahead. After that, a meal of venison and rice and a long, slow fuck. Life was good, for now.

Leon intended to keep it that way.

Chapter Eight

That evening, easing his aching body gingerly onto the bed, Leon decided he'd been severely underestimating Grim all this time. He'd watched Grim clean and gut fish, skin and dress rabbits, birds and deer, but he'd never appreciated what hard work it was. He'd assumed the whole thing was as easy as Grim made it look.

It wasn't. Raw flesh, Leon quickly discovered, was tough, and the ligaments and tendons holding the joints together even tougher. Grim's knives and cleavers were hefty and well-honed, so sharp that when Leon accidentally cut himself, he didn't even feel it, but it had still taken him a considerable amount of effort to separate the deer's legs from its body. He hadn't dared to help Grim skin the carcass after that. His injured shoulder had begun to ache, and his arms felt weak. He was afraid that if he tried to skin the animal, the knife would slip and he would cut himself again. Or worse, cut Grim.

"Sorry I wasn't more help," Leon said as Grim came back inside, arms wet to the elbows, carrying the dinner dishes he'd been washing in the little stream behind the cabin. "I'll get the hang of it eventually, I swear."

Grim smiled as he stacked the clean dishes on the hutch. Shadows from the failing light outside made his dimple seem deeper than normal. "You did fine, Leon. Especially for your first time. It'll get easier, don't worry." He grabbed a long match from the dwindling supply beside the woodbox, kindled it in the stove and lit the kerosene lantern. Carrying the lantern over to the bed, he placed it carefully on the floor and sat on the futon beside Leon. "Are you hurting? I can give you a massage, if you want."

Reaching up, Leon brushed the hair from Grim's eyes. "You don't have to do that. You must be tired too."

"Not really. I'm used to it. You're not." Grim slid both hands beneath Leon's sweater. His fingers were icy from the cold water of the stream, making Leon's skin pebble. "So, would you like a massage? Or would you rather have something else?"

The familiar gleam in Grim's eyes told Leon precisely what Grim meant by "something else". In an instant, Leon's fatigue was swept away by a wave of desire so intense it froze his breath.

Ignoring the way his sore muscles screamed at him, he locked his arms around Grim's waist and rolled so that Grim lay underneath him. Grim squeaked in surprise. He stared up at Leon with wide, lust-dark eyes, panting through parted lips. His hands clutched Leon's shoulders so hard it hurt.

"I want to fuck you," Leon said, his voice low and rough.

Grim's eyelids fluttered. His face flushed pink. "Okay. Will you let me up? So I can undress and...and everything?"

Leon shook his head. Every time they had sex, it was doggie-style. Grim hadn't said no on the one occasion when Leon had requested a different position, but he'd been so clearly uncomfortable fucking face-to-face that Leon had changed his mind.

Not that he didn't enjoy taking Grim from behind. He did. Very much. But he could no longer ignore his desire to watch Grim's face while they fucked, to look into his eyes when he came.

"Not yet," Leon whispered, drawing his fingers down Grim's cheek in a soft caress. "Just lie here for a little while. Let me touch you. Okay?"

The apprehension Leon had expected filled Grim's eyes, but it wasn't strong enough to drown out the need pouring off him in palpable waves. He nodded.

It was all the permission Leon needed. Standing up, Leon undressed as fast as he could. Grim lay still, his gaze raking up and down Leon's body. Naked, Leon knelt on the bed and started pulling off Grim's clothes. Grim tried to help. When Leon batted his hands away, he kept himself busy stroking as much of Leon's skin as he could reach.

Once he had Grim undressed, Leon nudged his legs apart and knelt between them. He reached over to the little bedside table Grim had built the previous month and grabbed the tub of cooking fat they'd started using when the lube ran out. The smell of it wasn't pleasant, but Leon figured that was a small price to pay for the pure bliss of sinking his cock into Grim's body.

Grim hadn't needed much preparation after their first few times together. At this point, a couple firm strokes of Leon's thumb was usually all it took for Grim's hole to open up. Normally, Leon would plunge his prick into Grim's ass the second the tight muscles relaxed enough. Tonight, he wanted to take his time. To touch and tease, caress Grim inside and out until all his inhibitions melted away and he gave himself up completely to Leon.

Fingers coated with grease, Leon scooted backward enough to bend forward and kiss the tip of Grim's cock. Grim let out a surprised shout and tried to squirm away. Leon stopped him with a hand across his hips.

"Relax," Leon murmured, pressing his cheek to the inside of Grim's thigh. He pushed two fingers into Grim's ass, drawing a ragged moan from Grim. "I want to suck your cock. Let me?"

He raised his head to look into Grim's eyes. Grim stared back, worrying his bottom lip between his teeth. He wanted Leon to do it. That much was clear on his face. Leon held his breath, hoping Grim would set aside his fear of making decisions in bed and tell Leon what he really wanted.

"Okay," Grim whispered finally. His eyes were huge, his breath coming far too fast.

Leon wanted Grim to say it. Hearing the words "suck my cock" from Grim's lips would be so fucking hot. But he kept the thought to himself. For some reason, this was a huge step for Grim, and Leon didn't want to push his luck.

Moving slowly, Leon took the tip of Grim's prick into his mouth and sealed his lips around it. He circled the silky-soft head with his tongue, dipping into the slit and under the edge of the foreskin. Grim moaned, legs spreading wider.

Humming, Leon took Grim deep into his throat. God, Grim tasted good, sharp and rich and earthy. Leon crooked his fingers to nail Grim's gland, just so he could feel Grim's body jerk and hear his soft whimpers.

"Oooooooh, God," Grim breathed as Leon pulled his fingers out, pushed both thumbs in and spread him open. "Good. Oh. Leon."

Grim's thighs shifted. Sliding his mouth up Grim's shaft to suck at the head, Leon glanced up, and nearly came right then. Grim's hands were hooked behind his knees, lifting his legs up and spreading them obscenely wide. His head was twisted to the side, mouth open and eyes screwed shut. He looked decadent and beautiful, and Leon's heart swelled with the knowledge that he was the one giving Grim such pleasure. It was a powerful feeling.

He worked Grim with lips, fingers and tongue until he heard the breathless "uh-uh-uh" sounds which usually preceded Grim's orgasms, then abruptly drew back. Grim's cock hit his belly with a damp smack as it popped free of Leon's mouth. Pulling his fingers free of Grim's hole, Leon rose to his knees between Grim's splayed legs.

Grim stared at Leon with unfocused eyes. "Wh... What? I...n-need... I need..." His words trailed off into a frustrated whine. Letting go of his right leg, he grabbed his cock, dug his foot into the mattress and thrust up into his hand. A low moan issued from his lips.

Leon drew a shaky breath and let it out, trying to hold on to his control. He'd never seen Grim completely incoherent before, and the sight was almost enough to undo him.

He leaned forward over Grim's body, planting his hands on either side of Grim's rib cage to hold his weight. His cock brushed Grim's, and they both groaned at the contact. "I can't see your face down there," Leon said, bending lower until he could feel Grim's short, sharp breaths on his lips. "I want you to come with my cock in your ass, and I want to watch your face when it happens."

Beneath him, Grim went tense and still. "N... Wh—? What?"

Grim's fear was obvious. The scent of it permeated the air. Leon had a feeling he had John to blame for this, too. What the fuck had the bastard done to make Grim so afraid of his own pleasure?

Anger surged through Leon's blood, but he held it in check, for Grim's sake. Shifting his weight to his right hand, he used his left to touch Grim's flushed cheek. "Don't be afraid," he whispered. "I won't make you do anything you don't want to, I promise. I just want to see you."

Grim turned his head, breaking eye contact. He didn't say anything, but the hitch in his breath and the tears gathering in his eyes announced his terror loud and clear. His cock began to soften against Leon's.

Leon had never felt more helpless in his life. Not knowing exactly what was wrong or how to fix it, he followed his instincts and did what he'd been longing to do for weeks. Cupping Grim's cheek in his hand, he closed the distance between them and pressed his lips to Grim's.

For a second, Grim lay stiff and unresponsive. Leon traced Grim's lower lip with the tip of his tongue, and the touch seemed to break Grim's paralysis. With a sigh that almost sounded like he was breathing Leon's name, Grim opened his mouth and tilted his head to seal their lips together.

The moment their tongues wound around one another, Leon knew Grim hadn't been kissed in a long, long time. He wasn't clumsy, he knew the mechanics of it, but he was shy and tentative in a way he never was during sex. Fucking was second nature to him. Kissing clearly was not.

Gotta fix that, Leon decided as Grim grew bolder, his tongue plunging deep to explore Leon's mouth. God, it was good, kissing Grim. Beyond good, in spite of Grim's inexperience. Amazing, transcendent, rapturous. Every superlative Leon had ever heard applied to this kiss. Sparks danced along his skin with each stroke of Grim's tongue against his. He felt drunk and dizzy, buoyed by a euphoria unlike any he'd experienced before.

Eventually, the insistent ache in his crotch forced him to break the kiss. He drew back enough to meet Grim's rather glazed eyes.

Grim looked stunned, as if he couldn't believe Leon had

really kissed him. He touched his fingertips to his lips. "Leon?"

"Hmm?" Dipping his head, Leon laid an open-mouthed kiss on Grim's throat.

Grim arched his neck and canted his hips upward. His erection was back, rubbing hard and hot against Leon's. "Fuck me? Please?"

"Like this?" Leon thrust his groin into Grim's, savoring the rough cry it elicited from Grim. "Face to face?"

"Yes. Yes. God." Grim bent his legs up, folding himself nearly in half to bring his ass in blazing contact with Leon's cock. "Fuck me. See me, God, Leon, please!"

As hot as it was when Grim begged to be fucked, his plea to be *seen* was what set off fireworks in Leon's belly.

He took hold of his cock, lined the head up with Grim's hole and pushed inside. Grim was loose and slick, and Leon's prick sank in to the hilt without resistance. Snug heat engulfed him, undulating around his shaft and setting his body on fire. He groaned.

"Fuck, you feel good," Leon gasped. Resting his weight on his elbows, he pulled partway out and plunged in again, angling up to hit Grim's gland.

Grim let out a keening cry. His long legs wrapped around Leon's waist, heels digging into his spine. He clenched both hands into Leon's hair and pulled. Before Leon knew what was happening, Grim's mouth was on his again, kissing him with bruising force.

The unexpected aggression ramped up Leon's arousal to a near-painful level. Growling into Grim's open mouth, Leon dug his knees into the futon and pounded into Grim's body with all his strength.

It wasn't what he'd planned. He'd wanted to take his time,

to show Grim the difference between fucking and making love. But Grim's lust was heady, infectious, and Leon couldn't fight it. He didn't *want* to fight it, especially when Grim so clearly wanted to be taken hard and fast.

Somewhere in the back of his brain, Leon realized the fear which normally kept Grim from fully letting go had been overcome by a kiss. *His* kiss. It amazed him that something so simple could make such a difference.

Grim's thighs tightened around him, desperate little noises bleeding from Grim's mouth to his. Leon had learned to read Grim's signals over the past weeks. He knew what those sweet noises meant. Shifting his weight without breaking the kiss, Leon angled his hips so he could hit Grim's prostate with ease on each thrust. Grim whimpered and shook underneath him. He responded by picking up the pace, slamming into Grim in short, quick jabs. The damp smack of their bodies slapping together and the musky tang of sex filled the room.

Grim's lips stopped moving, his mouth going slack against Leon's. His breath came in tiny gasps. He was close, and Leon wanted to push him over the edge and watch him fall. Hoping Grim would be too far gone to protest, he curled his fingers around Grim's cock and started pumping.

This time, Grim didn't tense, or try to move away, or replace Leon's hand with his own. He let out a long, ragged moan which shot through Leon like a lightning bolt. One leg uncurled from around Leon's waist and bent up so that his foot rested on Leon's shoulder. The movement tilted his hips enough that when Leon glanced down between them, he could see his cock sliding in and out of Grim's ass.

The sight was enough to bring Leon to the brink. He hung on, determined to make Grim come first. Right then, nothing seemed as important as witnessing the moment of Grim's release.

"That's it, kid," Leon panted, staring into Grim's sex-hazed eyes. "Let go. Show me."

Grim's eyes snapped into focus. For a second, his gaze bored into Leon, and it was like looking through a door which had been shut forever and had finally opened. Then he flung his head back and came with a wail. His body arched and bucked, nearly throwing Leon off. The leg still cinched around his waist and the sudden contraction of Grim's hole around his shaft were the only things keeping Leon in place.

Watching Grim lose himself like that was enough to tip the balance for Leon. He came deep inside Grim's ass, eyes wide open and fixed on Grim's face, and it was everything he'd ever wanted.

He managed to pull out and flop onto his back beside Grim rather than on top of him. They lay side by side in silence for a few minutes, breathing hard. When Grim moved to get up, to fetch a wet cloth as he always did to wash them both off, Leon laid a restraining hand on his wrist.

"Stay here," Leon said. "I'll get it."

Grim hunched his shoulders. "But I'm supposed to take care of you. That's how it works."

The matter-of-fact tone in which Grim said it, as if it were a given that he was a lower order of life, tore at Leon's heart. Sitting up, he pulled Grim into his arms and kissed him, a brief brush of lips meant to comfort rather than arouse. "Maybe that's how it worked with John." *That fucking bastard. If I ever find him, I'll cut his fucking heart out.* "But that's not how it works now, with me. If we're going to be together, we can't keep doing things the way we have been. I can't be your master, Grim. We have to be on equal footing. I can't do it any other way."

Grim stilled. His dark eyes searched Leon's face. Leon waited, feeling calmer than he would've thought after what he'd just said. He hadn't meant to put it quite that baldly. He'd only meant to remind Grim that he was Leon's lover, not his servant. But now that it was out—now that Grim knew Leon wanted more than just something to fuck—Leon felt a weight lifted from him. Every word he'd said, he meant, and there was no going back now.

If Grim couldn't accept Leon's terms, it would hurt, but Leon would get over it eventually. He'd survived worse.

When Grim lay back down without a word, it felt to Leon like the first step down the road toward something permanent. Smiling, he leaned over and kissed the end of Grim's nose, then hauled himself out of bed.

The room was warm, heated by the fire Grim kept going in the stove, but the floor was chilly on his bare feet. He walked over to the hutch, opened the bottom cabinet and found a clean washcloth and towel. Taking the washbasin down from the shelf, he poured some water into it from the bucket Grim kept beside the stove. He carried the basin, washcloth and towel across the room and set them on the bedside table.

The water was cold, so Leon rung the excess out of the cloth and warmed it between his hands before swabbing the drying semen off Grim's groin and belly. "Turn over," he said, rinsing the washcloth in the basin. "So I can wash your ass."

Grim rolled obediently onto his front. Head pillowed on his folded arms, he gave Leon a puzzled look. "I don't understand why you're doing this. Does it turn you on to wash me?"

It did, in a way, but Leon wasn't about to say so. This wasn't about sex. It was about making Grim see himself the way Leon saw him.

"This isn't a sex fantasy, no." Leon washed off the spunk

trickling from Grim's hole to smear the backs of his thighs. "This is me doing something nice for you because I want to, and because you deserve to have someone look after *you* for a change. That's all."

Grim's cheeks flushed, his lips parting. "Mmm. Feels good." The lustful glitter was back in Grim's eyes. His bottom raised off the bed, just enough for Leon to feel the motion.

Leon's eyebrows shot up. He grinned. "I think this is turning *you* on."

The muscles in Grim's back bunched as his body went tight. "I...I'm sorry. I'll—"

"You'll stay right there," Leon interrupted. Tossing the washcloth into the basin, he knelt in the V of Grim's legs and pushed his thighs farther apart. "I don't think I can get it up again, but there's other ways."

Twisting his torso around, Grim gave Leon a panicked look. "What do you mean? I don't need anything, honest!"

"Yes you do. And I don't ever want to hear you apologize for that." Leon leaned over to touch Grim's cheek. "You're young, of course you're gonna be able to get hard more often than I can. It's okay. I want to make you feel good. Just let me, huh?"

Grim covered his face with one hand. *You fucking idiot, you fucked it up already,* Leon berated himself. *Do something!*

The kiss earlier had taken Grim by surprise, and thus broken down one of the many walls between himself and any potential partner. Maybe, Leon mused, such a thing would work again. It was sure worth a try.

Planting his hands on Grim's ass cheeks, Leon spread them apart, bent and lapped at Grim's hole.

Grim let out a sharp cry. "Fuck! What are...you...? Oh, my God."

Clearly, Grim had never been on the receiving end of a rim job. Considering the sheer shock in his voice, Leon figured he probably hadn't even realized people did such things.

Pleased with himself, Leon stiffened his tongue and delved it into Grim's anus. Most of the cooking fat was gone, leaving behind only a trace of meaty taste which was nearly lost in the salty bitterness of semen and Grim's own unique flavor. Leon felt like he'd never get enough of Grim's rich, wonderful taste. The smell of come and well-fucked ass made him wish his cock would catch up to his brain and show a little more interest.

This isn't for you, asshole, he reminded himself, as Grim's hips bucked up against his face. *How many times has he gotten you off while he went without? This is for him. Just for him.*

Grim tucked his knees underneath him and raised his ass into the air. Leon rose with him, sliding a hand between the boy's legs to stroke his renewed erection while his tongue bathed Grim's insides as far as it could reach. Grim didn't even seem aware of his own wanton movements, or his soft "oh, oh, oh," chanting. His hips rocked in a constant back-and-forth, fucking himself on Leon's tongue with one motion and shoving his prick through the circle of Leon's hand with the other.

When Grim's hole fluttered against his tongue and his shaft swelled in his hand, Leon knew Grim was about to come. Moving as fast as he could, Leon pulled his tongue out of Grim's ass, wriggled underneath him and gulped his cock down, shoving two fingers deep inside him to massage his gland.

"Oooooh, oh God!" Grim cried, and came in a hot, slippery trickle down Leon's throat. Leon swallowed, wishing he could've fed on the far more copious load Grim had shot all over his stomach mere minutes ago.

Next time, he promised himself, suckling the last of Grim's semen from his twitching cock.

He moved just in time to avoid being trapped when Grim collapsed into a trembling heap. Grim stared at Leon, looking dazed and more than a little awestruck.

Lying down beside Grim, Leon wrapped the boy's shaking body in his arms and held him close, stroking his hair. "You okay?"

Grim nodded. To Leon's relief, Grim curled himself around Leon's body and laid his head on his chest. "I didn't know people could do that," Grim said, his voice low and tremulous. He wound an arm around Leon's middle. "Is it always like this? When people are...you know, together?"

Somehow, Leon knew Grim wasn't asking about the rim job. "Not always. But it *should* be." He rested his cheek against Grim's damp hair. "If you lo...care about somebody, you don't want to be selfish. You want to make them happy. You know?"

If Grim noticed what Leon had almost said, he didn't let on. He cuddled closer, yawning. "God, I'm tired. I should get up before I fall asleep."

Leon tightened his arms around Grim before he could move. "Don't go back to that stupid sleeping bag. Stay here, with me."

He'd been wanting to extend that particular invitation for a while. He'd restrained himself because he knew it would make Grim uncomfortable. Now, asking Grim to share the bed with him seemed like the most natural thing in the world.

To his relief, Grim seemed to agree. With a sweet smile, Grim raised up and pressed a light kiss to Leon's lips, then settled back into Leon's embrace. Within seconds, he was sound asleep, his breathing deep and even, his body warm and relaxed against Leon's chest.

Leon wanted to stay awake and savor the feel of Grim sleeping in his arms. But hard work, harder revelations and some of the best sex he'd ever had combined into a force Leon couldn't fight. His eyes closed in spite of himself, and sleep sucked him in.

$$\wp$$

Leon woke in moonlit darkness. He lay still, surveying his surroundings from under half-closed eyelids.

Everything seemed perfectly normal. Outside, the wind howled through the trees. Rain pelted against the windows. In the little room, nothing stirred. Beside him, Grim lay curled in a ball, the curve of his bare back pressed against Leon's side.

Leon frowned, wondering what had woken him. He didn't sense any danger, but something was definitely off. The air felt tense and brittle, as if some sound or movement had recently disturbed the stillness.

Just as Leon decided to get up and check the cabin—and grab a knife, just in case—Grim's body jerked so violently he nearly knocked Leon into the wall. His heel connected with Leon's shin hard enough to make Leon hiss in pain.

So that's what woke me up. Leaning over, Leon brushed the hair away from Grim's face. Whatever was going on in his head, it must've been terrifying. Grim's brow was furrowed, his mouth twisted in a grimace of fear. Tears leaked from his tightly closed eyes, sparkling in the moonlight where they caught on his lashes. He didn't make a sound, but his hands kept pushing at something only he could see, and tremors shook his body.

Leon had no idea what to do. Ted was the only person he'd ever actually slept with before now, and Ted had never once had a nightmare. Not knowing what else to do, Leon molded himself to Grim's back, wound an arm around his waist and kissed his cheek.

"Grim," he murmured. "Wake up. You're having a bad dream."

Grim didn't wake, but his trembling eased and the lines of fear smoothed from his face. He relaxed in Leon's embrace, still sleeping, the nightmare evidently gone. Beneath Leon's palm, Grim's racing heartbeat slowed to a more normal level. His skin was glazed with sweat, in spite of the chill in the room now that the fire in the woodstove had burned low.

Leon lay there, wide awake, staring at a bar of silver moonlight on the floor and pondering all the things he'd tried his best to avoid thinking of for the past six weeks. Something told him this wasn't Grim's first nightmare. And he thought he knew what in Grim's past—or rather, *who* in Grim's past—was the major contributor to his nighttime terrors.

True, Grim had jumped to John's defense earlier. But that didn't mean anything. How many women protested their abuser's innocence in spite of glaring evidence to the contrary? Leon still remembered every single time his mother had insisted his father had never meant to hurt her, even though her clothes were torn and her split lips caused the words to slur. Her swollen, blackened eyes were always so sincere it made Leon want to hit her himself. He figured any abusive relationship probably worked the same way.

He had no proof that John had ever abused Grim, but everything pointed to it. Grim's sexual skill, when he'd lived in the Alaskan forest since he was a young teen. His moments of cringing fear when he thought Leon was angry. His refusal to talk about his past in general, or John in particular. All the bits and pieces added up to a conclusion which turned Leon's stomach, but which he knew in his gut was true.

I'll tell every paper in this country about that boy in Portland

AND the one I know you're keeping now. Wallins' note had made it all gel for Leon. The faceless John must have brought Grim to this place for his own twisted pleasures, kept him until he no longer met the bastard's needs, and left him here.

Leon rubbed his cheek on Grim's. The boy's sparse stubble rasped against his skin. The hairs were fine and soft. Leon's beard hadn't felt like that since he was sixteen. It made Grim seem even younger than he was, and a wave of rage roared through Leon's blood. Rage at John, for taking Grim's life in a way worse than all Leon's murders put together. *If I ever get my hands on that fucker, I'll strangle him with his own intestines.*

Grim let out a tiny, distressed sound and shifted in Leon's arms. Realizing he was clutching Grim a little too tightly, Leon relaxed his grip. He nuzzled Grim's hair, breathing in the sour scent of fear-induced sweat.

When Grim settled into quiet sleep once again, Leon carefully unwound himself and climbed out of bed. His brain was going a mile a minute, and the pictures it presented him were not conducive to rest.

Without the blankets, the room was downright cold. Padding silently to the dresser, Leon opened each drawer in turn, looking for the clean sweats he knew were there someplace. It made him feel soiled to wear John's abandoned clothes, after finally coming to terms with what he was sure the fucker had done, but there wasn't really any choice.

The bottom drawer gave a faint squeak when Leon eased it open. The sound seemed unnaturally loud in the stillness. Leon glanced sideways at Grim. The kid hadn't moved a muscle. Letting out a relieved breath, Leon knelt on the floor and dug through the clothes. They were as orderly as the rest of the place, every garment neatly folded, and Leon soon found the huge, heavy sweatshirt and sweatpants he'd been looking for.

As he lifted them out, a large black spider crawled out of a fold in the shirt. Startled, Leon dropped both garments on the floor. The spider scurried beneath the dresser.

Leon cursed under his breath. He fucking *hated* spiders. Pushing the clothes out of the way, he bent to peer under the dresser, intent on squashing the eight-legged intruder. The thing was nowhere in sight, of course. They always seemed to vanish into thin air. But there *was* something underneath the piece of heavy furniture, standing upright between the dresser and the wall. Leon could only see the bottom of it, but it looked like a book.

Leon frowned. *Grim can't read. And even if he could, why would he keep a book behind the dresser?*

Curious, he moved to the side of the dresser and slid his arm into the narrow space. Almost at the limit of his reach, he snagged the book between two fingers and drew it out. He held it up to look at it.

What he saw was a hardcover, spiral bound notebook. He couldn't be sure of the color—something dark, with no pattern or decoration—but it didn't matter anyway. What mattered was the single word emblazoned across the top in large, stark white block letters.

Journal.

Grim couldn't read, which meant he couldn't write either. It wasn't his journal, and there was only one other person who it could have belonged to.

Leon stared at the diary, torn between the desire to throw it against the wall in disgust and the nearly overwhelming need to read it. To *know*, finally, what Grim had endured during his years here with John.

In the end, the need to know won. Shoving to his feet, Leon pulled the clothes on as fast as he could. A quick search of the hutch turned up an old stub of a candle. Leon lit it from the embers in the stove and settled onto Grim's sleeping bag on the floor to read.

Chapter Nine

When the first thin light of day crept through the windows, Leon was still sitting there, staring at the flickering candle flame. John's diary lay closed on the floor beside him.

It hadn't been comfortable reading. Hell, the damn book had not only confirmed his fears, it had opened up whole new realms of nightmare fodder. The sex—starting when Grim was fourteen, God, just a baby—wasn't even the worst of it. The thing that made the bile rise in Leon's throat was the way John had manipulated Grim, mostly through veiled threats of starvation and abandonment, into consenting to it all.

I have never once forced my attentions on the boy. I take great pride in this. Even Grim's punishments have been dealt to him only once he agreed that they were necessary. Of course, he is reluctant to have me touch him, especially sexually. He hides it well, but I see his fear, and his disgust. But I give him food and shelter, and hide him from the authorities. It's only fair he should give me his body in return. It is all I ask. I feel it a reasonable exchange, when I have given up everything to bring him here, and keep him safe.

It was the one passage which haunted Leon the most. John's belief in his own innocence threaded through the entire journal, but that one paragraph laid it all on the table. The bastard truly believed he'd saved Grim somehow, and he'd convinced Grim of that as well. Worse, he knew what he was doing to Grim, but thought his behavior was justified because he'd rescued Grim from some kind of trouble with the law.

"Probably shoplifting or something," Leon muttered. He rubbed both hands over his face. "Fuck."

Across the room, Grim stirred. "Leon?" Yawning, he pushed up on one elbow and ran a hand through his tangled hair. "Why are you over there?"

Staring into Grim's sleepy, trusting eyes, Leon wanted to lie. He didn't know shit about abuse victims, but he knew about betrayal, and he was willing to bet Grim would feel betrayed if he found out what Leon had spent the better part of the night reading. Betrayed and angry.

"I've never seen you angry," Leon said, half to himself.

Grim's brows drew together. "What?"

You have to tell him you read this, asshole. Just fucking do it.

Shut up. I'll get to it.

"You don't ever get angry. Never. Except that one time, when I called John selfish." Blowing out the candle, Leon crossed to the bed and sat beside Grim. "What he did to you was wrong. You have to know that."

Grim's expression grew wary. "I'd really rather not talk about John, if that's okay."

"No. It's not okay." Leon leaned over and stopped the protest he knew was coming with a kiss. When he pulled back, he laid his fingers on Grim's lips. *So soft.* "I found John's diary behind the dresser. I spent the last few hours reading it."

In a heartbeat, Grim's body went still and tense. He didn't speak, and he wouldn't meet Leon's gaze. Leon pressed on, determined to get the whole fucking mess out in the open once and for all.

"He knew what he was doing to you, Grim. He knew it was wrong. But he didn't care. He thought you owed him, because he hid you from the cops." Leon raked the hair from Grim's face. He wished Grim would look at him. "He used you. He forced you to do all those things, and made you think you agreed to it. I bet he even tricked you into coming here with him in the first place." The journal hadn't detailed precisely how John had gotten Grim to come to this remote wilderness. He'd mentioned meeting Grim almost in passing, saying he'd found the boy running from the police and offered him a place to stay.

"He didn't trick me." Grim's voice was calm, but full of a hardness Leon had never heard from him before. "I wanted him to take me away. I would've done anything."

"And he took advantage of that, when he knew it was wrong." Leon ran a fingertip down Grim's cheek. "You were just a kid, you were scared, and he used that. Whatever you did to get in trouble with the law, it couldn't have been that bad."

To Leon's shock, Grim shoved him away, scrambled to his feet and stood staring down at Leon with a fine, hot fury blazing in his eyes. "You don't know a fucking thing about it. Not a *thing.*"

Leon forced back his automatic surge of anger. If he couldn't control his temper, he'd lose Grim for good, and he didn't think he could stand that. "What'd you do, steal something? What teenager doesn't lift a game or a CD or something at least once? You didn't need to—"

"Oh, yes I did." Grim laughed, the sound sharp and bitter. "I've stolen plenty of things. But I never got caught. The cops weren't after me for shoplifting. I needed a place to hide, and John gave me that."

Something in the set of Grim's mouth and the dark glitter

in his eyes sent a hard chill down Leon's spine. "So what'd you do?"

For a second, Leon thought Grim might actually tell him. He barely swallowed a frustrated growl when Grim shook his head and turned to gaze out the back window. "Doesn't matter now. John offered me a way out, and I took it. That's all."

He doesn't want to tell me what he did. Fine. There's still the subject of that fucking waste of space John to clear up.

"Where's John now?" Leon asked, watching the tight muscles ripple in Grim's back. God, the boy was so tense he looked ready to explode.

"Why do you care?"

Leon blinked, surprised by the venom in Grim's tone. This was a morning of firsts, evidently. It was a relief, in a way. Direct confrontation was something Leon knew how to deal with, even if he didn't always handle it particularly well. He had no idea what to do with Grim's usual veneer of happiness, since it hid the most fucked-up soul Leon had ever encountered.

"I care, because if he shows his face around here, I'll kill him. I know you don't think he did anything to you, but I know he did, and if I ever catch him, he's gonna die."

Grim hung his head. His hair spilled over his shoulders to bare a long line of pale neck. "John's already dead. He died a couple of months before you showed up."

Leon sighed. He'd been afraid of this. Afraid Grim would make up some new story to cover John's departure, and to keep Leon from killing the bastard.

Standing, Leon went to Grim and wrapped both arms around his waist. "He's not dead, Grim. He abandoned you."

Grim shook his head. "No. I found him in the woods. I buried him."

What he had to say was going to sound horribly harsh, but Leon couldn't make himself sugarcoat it. Grim had to face the fact that John was a monster.

"It's all in his diary," Leon said, pressing a kiss to Grim's bare shoulder. His chest felt tight, knowing this whole conversation was hurting Grim. "The last entry said he was done with you, that you were too old to satisfy him anymore and he was going to find some other victim."

Grim moved so fast Leon didn't even know what was happening until he found himself flat on his back, Grim straddling his hips, hands clamped around his neck. He grabbed Grim's wrists, pried at his fingers, but couldn't loosen the boy's iron grip without harming him. Leon stared at Grim, impressed in spite of his situation. He'd never have thought the kid had it in him.

"I am not a victim!" Grim shouted, thumbs pressing painfully into Leon's windpipe. "John took care of me. He was the only one who *ever* took care of me, and fuck you if you can't see that!" He shook Leon like a rag doll, banging his head on the floor. "He's dead, I buried him myself, all by myself because there wasn't anybody else, there's *never* been anybody else! And I, I thought...I thought you..."

Grim trailed off, but Leon's mind filled in the rest. *Grim thought you'd be like John, be his absolute master. He thought you'd take care of him like John did, and he thought you would use him like John did. He thinks that's the only way anyone could ever care about him.*

The revelation hurt something deep in Leon's soul, but he didn't have the luxury of focusing on that right now. Grim's grip on Leon's throat was growing tighter. His vision sparkled and his head pounded, static hissing in his ears. He didn't want to hurt Grim, but at this point there wasn't much choice. If he didn't do something, right now, Grim was going to choke him to death. Grim's face was ghostly white, wide eyes gleaming with fury and fear and a hopelessness that twisted Leon's heart.

With the last of his strength, Leon slammed his forearms into Grim's elbows. Grim let out a grunt, and his fingers slipped from Leon's throat. Leon shoved him, sending him tumbling backward.

At the same time, Leon heard a muffled pop from behind him. Grim jerked as he fell, and something warm and wet sprinkled Leon's leg. Gasping for breath, he turned toward the direction where he'd heard the pop. A gunshot, he belatedly realized as a man and woman dressed in green and black camouflage rushed into the room, weapons drawn to cover both himself and Grim.

Grim. Oh, God.

Chapter Ten

"Grim," Leon rasped, pushing himself to a sitting position. He ignored the shouts to freeze, stay down, don't fucking move, and crawled to where Grim lay shivering on the floor. Blood leaked from a bullet hole in his chest—too high up to have hit his heart, thank God—and pooled on the floor.

"L...Le...on. S-sorry." Grim stopped, panting. His teeth chattered. An ominous whistling sound accompanied each breath he drew.

Alarmed, Leon laid his palm over the bullet wound. The whistling stopped. "Grim. Oh fuck."

"Step away from him," a hard female voice ordered. "Hands on top of your head."

Leon raised his free hand slowly into the air, palm open, but didn't move his other hand. "His lung's punctured. You have to get him to a hospital." He managed to hold back the urge to call her a brainless cunt. The last thing he or Grim needed right now was for him to get shot too.

"Not gonna happen, Fisher." The woman's voice was cold and clipped. "Take your hand off his chest, lace both hands behind your head and stand up, nice and slow."

Leon stared at Grim's pale face, at the brown eyes full of a horrible resignation, and realized he'd rather die right here than live with knowing he'd killed Grim just as surely as if he'd pulled the trigger himself.

"No," Leon heard himself say, as if from a great distance. "I won't leave him. Either he goes with us and you get him some help, or you can just kill me right now."

A heartbeat of silence, followed by low whispers. Leon risked a glance over his shoulder. The woman's gaze and her gun were both trained on Leon while she and her male companion held a hissing argument. Finally, the man glared at Leon and trotted out the door.

"Green's gone to get the Jeep," the woman told him. "He'll radio for a medical helicopter to meet us at the rendevous point."

Leon tried not to let his elation show on his face. Obviously, they were under orders to bring him back alive or else. Otherwise they would never have agreed to take the risk of helping Grim.

Leaning down, Leon brushed his lips across Grim's brow. His skin was grayish and cool, beaded with sweat. "Hang on, okay?" Leon whispered. "Help's coming."

Grim's eyes rolled up to meet Leon's. The deep brown was cloudy, hazed with pain. "L-Le...don't l-leave...Leon..."

The wet rasp of Grim's voice made dread coil in Leon's belly. Ignoring the woman's warning to stop, Leon let his upraised hand fall. He cupped Grim's cheek, tilted his head up and kissed his cold lips. "I won't leave you."

Grim's mouth curved into a faint smile. Nodding, he closed his eyes. If it hadn't been for the shallow hitch of his chest as he breathed, Leon might've thought he was dead.

Ignoring the nameless woman with the high-caliber pistol trained on him, Leon rested his forehead against Grim's hair. He could smell Grim's blood, his sweat and his terror. The boy's heart fluttered against Leon's palm, faint and far too fast.

Outside, the sound of a motor cut through the early morning stillness. As the motor stopped and footsteps pounded up to the cabin door, Leon shut his eyes and thought out to God, or Allah, or any of the dozens of other deities in which he didn't believe.

Please, let him be okay. Please.

⁐

The next few hours passed in a shock-hazed blur. Single moments caught like snapshots in Leon's brain. Grim lying white-faced and limp in the backseat of the Jeep, his head in Leon's lap. The clearing in the forest, so fucking far away, the trees lashing each other with their branches as the helicopter swooped down from the glowering clouds. People all around, strangers, taking Grim from his arms. Handcuffs biting into his wrists, Green and the woman hauling him into the helicopter, buckling him in and leaving.

He didn't wonder how they'd found Grim's cabin, or why they hadn't climbed into the helicopter too. Later, he'd have his answers. If Grim died, his revenge would be terrible. But right now, he didn't care. Not when the person who had become his whole world lay bleeding on a narrow stretcher, his life in the hands of the same people who had put him there.

They were Jones' people. Green, the woman, the medics in the helicopter, all of them. Leon was certain of it. Every move they made screamed their connection to the organization Jones represented.

The helicopter landed on the roof of what looked like a hospital in the middle of a small city which sprouted like a multicolored fungus between the forest and a wide channel of blue-gray water. Four nurses met them with a gurney. Grim was whisked away, down an elevator to what damn well better be the best medical care in the whole fucking country.

The man who'd watched Leon with dead shark's eyes in the helicopter grasped Leon's arm and led him to a stairwell on the other side of the roof. Leon was taken down one flight and along a hallway to a room with a sign on the door reading "Family Conference". It contained two plush chairs, a small sofa and a table strewn with outdated magazines. The man shoved Leon inside and locked him in with his wrists still cuffed behind his back.

He stayed there for what seemed like days but couldn't have been more than three or four hours. The clouds had settled in and opened up, veiling the city behind a watery gray curtain. With nothing more productive to do, Leon stared out the window and watched the rain, trying to keep his mind blank.

It didn't work. By the time the door opened and Jones strolled in carrying a thin manila folder, Leon's worry and anger had reached the boiling point. He glared at her, barely holding back the urge to jump up and scream in her face.

"Mr. Fisher," she greeted him, cool as if he hadn't been MIA for the last six weeks. "How wonderful to see you alive after all."

Leon shifted forward in his seat, wriggling his fingers to get some circulation going. "Where's Grim? Is he all right?"

One manicured eyebrow lifted. "The boy White shot? The one who was attempting to strangle you, or so I am led to believe?"

White. Must be the woman. He scowled. "I had it under control, dammit, she didn't have to shoot him."

Jones crossed the room and lowered herself into the second chair, laying the folder on the table atop an old copy of *Newsweek.* "Green and White both tell me your behavior toward

133

this boy was...unexpected."

"That's none of your fucking business," Leon growled. "Just tell me if he's okay."

"He will have to remain in the hospital for a while, but he is expected to make a full recovery." Crossing her legs, she picked a bit of lint off her skirt. "You realize, of course, that we will have to turn him over to the proper authorities as soon as he is well enough. If we'd been able to treat the boy at the lake house, perhaps it could have been avoided. But a hospital is, I'm afraid, quite a public place. Attempting to hide him could very well expose the organization, and I can't allow that."

Something cold and ugly curled in Leon's gut. "What's he wanted for?"

She smiled. "He didn't tell you? Oh my. Such secrets to keep from one's lover."

I will not kill her. I will not kill her. "Jones. Just tell me. What's he wanted for?"

"Murder, actually. He shot a man in Anchorage. A drug deal gone bad, evidently. The man he killed was the son of a prominent local politician. You can imagine the scandal." She clasped her hands around her knee and pinned Leon with a penetrating stare. "This young man with whom you've become so infatuated is a killer, Mr. Fisher. Just like you."

Leon leaned back in the chair and shut his eyes. Grim, a murderer. Just like him.

No. *Not* just like him. He'd gone into the assassination business with eyes wide open, knowing exactly what he was getting into. He'd killed without remorse, and slept well at night. Grim wasn't like that. If it was true, if he'd really shot someone when he was fourteen, it must have left deep scars. It must haunt him.

"He was just a kid." Leon opened his eyes and glared at

Jones, as if Grim's past were her fault. He wished it was. It would've been nice to have someone to blame. "How do you know it's even him the cops are after? He's been out there in the fucking forest for six years. He practically grew up there, for Christ's sake. How do you know it's him?"

In answer, Jones picked up the folder, rifled through it and pulled out a single piece of paper and held it up for Leon to see.

It was a "Wanted" poster. Across the top were two black and white pictures of a disheveled and sullen-looking boy, one from the front and one in profile. The kid in the picture was younger and harder looking, but it was unquestionably Grim. Beneath the mug shot was a short but damning paragraph.

Holmes, Graham. Birth date unknown. Wanted for murder in the May 4, 2000 shooting of Cassidy Banks. Subject is described as a Caucasian male, age approximately fourteen years, approximately five feet ten inches tall, weighing approximately one hundred forty-five pounds. Last seen in the area of Fairview Lions Park on the night in question, talking to an older man in a dark blue sedan. Holmes is a member of the infamous Death Squad, the gang behind last year's wave of deadly carjackings. Anyone with information on Graham Holmes' whereabouts, contact the Municipality of Anchorage sheriff's department.

There was more. Phone numbers, a case number, a list of prior arrests. But none of that mattered. Right here in black and white was the proof that Grim was indeed wanted by the police, even if it didn't prove he'd actually committed the crime.

"There's no mistake," Jones said, sounding infuriatingly smug. "Your young bedmate murdered a man, and fled into the wilderness to avoid capture." She lowered the paper and returned it to the folder. "You see how it is, Mr. Fisher. There is no statute of limitations on murder. We must turn the boy in or risk being exposed ourselves."

135

Leon stared at her, keeping his face impassive. The wheels were already turning in his head, working out a way to get Grim out of here as soon as possible. He couldn't betray that to Jones. He had to play along, for now.

"I want to see him," Leon demanded, knowing Jones expected it. She wouldn't allow it, he knew. If he ever wanted to see Grim again, he would need every ounce of his stealth and cunning.

"Perhaps." Her dark eyes glittered. "He will not be fit to receive visitors for several days yet. But I will see what I can do."

Yeah, I bet you will. Leon let a little fake relief bleed into his eyes. "Good. I'd be dead if it weren't for him, you know."

"We assumed as much, yes."

Leon turned away from Jones' unrevealing face to stare out the window. "How'd you find me, anyway?"

"At first, we were looking for your body. Your backpack was found many miles from the lake house, in another lake altogether. A park ranger recovered it, and the lake house being the only dwelling for a couple hundred square miles, he brought it there to see if the staff could identify it."

"And based on that, they decided I was dead?"

"The pack was torn and bloodstained, and battered almost to pieces. Only one river empties into the small lake where your pack was found, and that river contains many miles of class five rapids. An injured man couldn't possibly survive, or so we thought."

Leon shook his head, turning to look at Jones again. "So when did you figure out I wasn't dead and start looking for me?"

"Two weeks after you disappeared, the remains of a campsite were discovered alongside the river, high up in the mountains. We'd been unable to locate your body. We had to assume the campsite was yours." She pursed her lips. "The trail was cold by then, of course, and finding one man in that forest is nearly impossible. We were ready to give you up for lost after all, when one of my people picked up a transmission from a Tongass ranger station, reporting a poaching deep in the forest. We didn't *know* it was you, but this forest is utterly uninhabited. Or at least everyone believed that to be the case. It was worth looking into."

"Hell of a way to 'look into' the possibility," Leon observed, keeping his anger out of his voice with an effort. "Busting down the door and shooting a naked, unarmed kid."

"Green and White infiltrated the area the same day the poaching was reported. White is an accomplished tracker. She was able to follow the trail of deer's blood to the cabin. You were spotted and identified. She and Green radioed me for instructions. You know the rest."

Yes, he knew. He figured he'd see Grim bleeding on the cabin floor for the rest of his life, every time he shut his eyes.

Rising to her feet, Jones retrieved her folder and walked toward the door. "I am sorry about the handcuffs, Mr. Fisher, but it was necessary. We had to tell the hospital management something, so we told them we were bringing in two criminals, one of whom was injured, and would need a secure spot to hold the one not wounded." She reached the door, turned and gave him a humorless smile. "Besides, I suspect you would have attacked me the moment I walked in if you weren't restrained, correct?"

Leon saw no point in lying. She knew him too well. "Yes."

"I would have regretted having to kill you."

"Like hell you would."

"Someone will be in shortly to take you to our Juneau base

of operations," Jones said. "I will speak with you again there."

Leon stood, though he didn't go any closer. "Grim thought the people at the lake house would've killed me if I went back there. Would they?"

Jones just smiled. "Good day, Mr. Fisher."

She walked out without another word. Leon stood gazing into space for a long time, thinking. Maybe Grim was right. Maybe they would've killed him. Maybe they were only looking for him in order to dispose of him properly. Just because they'd brought him here alive instead of shooting him in the forest meant nothing. Jones always did have her own mysterious ways of doing things. If she planned on disposing of him after all, he had only a limited amount of time in which to act.

First things first. He had to find out exactly how badly Grim was hurt, and when he'd be able to participate in his own rescue. There was no point in taking Grim out of here if moving him would endanger his life.

Once they have you at their headquarters, you'll never get out. You have to get away from them before they get you there.

Sinking back into the chair, Leon shut his eyes and started to lay his plans. By the time the stony-faced man from the helicopter showed up, Leon knew what to do. Letting his shoulders slump as if in exhaustion, or perhaps defeat, Leon let the man lead him out into the hallway.

&

They'd been in the plain gray car for nearly twenty minutes, but hadn't gotten more than a few miles from the hospital. According to whoever was on the other end of Stone Face's radio, there was a three car pileup at a major intersection a couple miles up from where they sat.

Leon had to stifle a grin. It couldn't have worked out better if he'd planned it that way. Sitting slumped against the window, Leon continued to feign sleep while watching Stony and the driver through slitted eyelids.

"Copy that," Stony said into the radio. "Over and out." He prodded Leon with his foot. "Open your eyes, Fisher."

"Hmm? What?" Leon blinked his eyes open, hoping he sounded as groggy as he intended to. "What's going on?"

He knew what was going on, having overheard Stony's conversation. Headquarters was just ahead, down a side street half a block away. With traffic gridlocked in all directions, they didn't dare bring him out of the car handcuffed and held at gunpoint. Too many witnesses, too many potential avenues of exposure.

They would have to remove the handcuffs. It was an advantage Leon hadn't expected to have, but he'd gladly take it.

"I know you weren't asleep. Turn around."

Stony's voice brooked no argument. Leon obediently turned around, holding his hands out behind him. The metal pressed hard into Leon's wrist bones for a moment as Stony opened the lock. The cuffs sprang open.

"Turn back around and lace your hands on top of your head."

Again Leon obeyed. He glanced at the man beside him. The muzzle of Stony's Glock was aimed so that any bullet fired would penetrate his rib cage and tear a hole in his heart. "Why all this? The cuffs and the gun? What're you afraid of?"

The taunt had no effect on old Stone Face. Leon hadn't expected it to, really.

"When the car stops, you stay put," Stony said, cold gaze

139

never wavering. "Brown there will get out first and open the door for you. You get out and stay put while I get out. I'll have my gun on you, even if nobody else can see it, so don't do anything stupid."

Leon sneered. "Don't worry, I'll be a good little prisoner. Jones has me by the short hairs, or didn't she tell you that?"

"Yeah, she told me." Stony laughed. It sounded rusty, like his throat wasn't used to making that sort of sound. "You fucking queers are all alike. Soft."

Stopping himself from lurching across the seat and breaking Stony's neck was surprisingly easy. In his mind's eye, Leon saw Grim lying in the hospital, alone and afraid, thinking Leon had abandoned him. Grim needed him. That was enough to make Leon keep his cool. He met his guardian's gaze with icy calm.

Stony seemed disappointed by Leon's lack of response. He scowled, but didn't say anything.

A few seconds later, the car turned down a narrow one-way street and rolled to a halt beside a building identical to every other building they'd passed for the last few blocks. The traffic here was nearly as heavy as it was on the main road, due to the sheer number of people trying to escape the gridlock.

"All right," Stony said. "We're here. You do one fucking thing I don't like, I'll kill you quicker than you can say Jack Robinson. Got it?"

Jack Robinson? Leon grinned. "You sound like my grandma."

Stony's face turned a dangerous shade of red. Leon held his breath. He shouldn't have been able to rattle Stone Face this badly, but there it was.

There weren't many times when a guy could actually use homophobia in his favor. This was one of those times. With any
140

luck, Stony would make his escape a little bit easier.

Sure enough, as the driver got out of the car and shut the door, Stony shoved the pistol into the side of Leon's head. It was a stupid move, the very one Leon had been hoping the man would make.

Quick as thought, Leon slammed his elbow into Stony's gun arm. Stony hissed, the Glock's aim wavering. Ducking out of the way, Leon clamped both hands around Stony's wrist and smashed the gun into his face.

"Fuck!" Stony shouted, voice garbled by his broken nose. "Brown!"

Leon didn't spare the time to look and see if Brown had heard. The car was most likely soundproofed, anyway. He snatched the gun from Stony's hand, aimed and fired in one smooth motion. Blood and brains sprayed the window behind Stony's shattered head. He slumped against the black leather seat.

Leon scooted as close as he could to the car door, ready to hop out the second Brown opened it. Stony's death had been silent, thanks to the highly illegal suppressor on his gun, and the tinted windows had probably hidden the drama in the car from the people driving by. Leon had no intention of killing Brown. Too many potential witnesses crawling past in their cars. Brown himself would make sure no one else discovered Stony's corpse. Jones and her bosses wouldn't tolerate it.

Leon flipped on the gun's safety and curled the barrel up against his wrist just as the door opened. Leon hopped out before Brown could see past him into the car. He let the overly long sleeve of his sweatshirt fall down over his hand, hiding the pistol.

Brown stepped back from the door. Leon stood beside him, face set into his best docile expression. After a few seconds, it became apparent that Stony wasn't getting out. Brown shot a threatening glare at Leon, then edged closer to the open car door.

"Sir?" he called. "You okay?"

No answer. Eyes narrowed in suspicion, Brown pointed a warning finger at Leon. "Don't you fucking move."

Leon widened his eyes and shook his head, as if to say, *Who, me?*

Moving sideways in order to keep Leon in sight, Brown drew his weapon and leaned down to look in the car. His jaw went slack. "Jesus H. Christ."

For one critical second, Brown's full attention was on the bloodbath in the car. It was all the opening Leon needed. Letting Stony's pistol slide down into his grip, he thumbed off the safety and fired two shots in rapid succession. One hit Brown in his gun hand, sending his pistol skittering under the car. The other hit his ankle. The bone splintered with an audible crack.

Brown's mouth stretched wide in a silent scream. Planting one bare foot on Brown's hip, Leon shoved him into the car atop the body of his dead cohort and slammed the door.

Leon was already at the end of the side street and turning the corner back the way they'd come when he heard the car door open behind him. There were no outraged cries, no threats, certainly no gunshots. Brown wouldn't dare risk it, even if he could manage to follow Leon with his shattered ankle. He'd be forced to call Jones for backup. By the time help arrived, Leon would be long gone. Years of practice made blending into a city, any city, second nature to him.

Leon snickered as he threaded his way through the cars to the other side of the street and took off running down the sidewalk, the Glock once again hidden in his sleeve. If he knew

Jones, Stone Face would end up being the lucky one here. He was already dead.

Five blocks down the road, Leon came to an intersection with another major avenue. He followed it west, away from where he knew the hospital lay. As much as he wanted to go back right now, find Grim and hold him and let him know they were leaving this place, soon, together, he knew he couldn't. Not yet. To do so right now would be suicide, and without him, Grim would be utterly alone in the world.

It was a strange feeling, being needed like that. Being important, not because of his skills with a weapon, but because of who he was. Grim had never said it, but Leon knew it was true anyway.

Grim needed him. They needed each other, and it felt good.

Leon grimaced when his foot landed in a puddle of icy water. His feet were so cold they ached, and the rain had soaked right through the sweats he wore. His stomach rumbled, reminding him that he hadn't eaten since the night before at Grim's cabin, a lifetime ago. He needed dry clothes, shoes and food, and preferably a place to hole up and think. But first, he needed money.

He glanced around, looking for a likely mark. Up ahead, a young woman strolled through the rain, a bright green umbrella in one hand and an open book in the other. A purple backpack with a Ninja on it hung down almost to her slim hips. The front pocket was only partly zipped.

Bingo.

Sidling up behind her, Leon eased the zipper open, reached inside and snatched out a folding wallet in blinding pink. He rolled the top of his sweatpants over the wallet and hurried into the nearest ally.

The wallet contained two twenties and a few crumpled

ones. It was enough, for now. Rolling the cash into his pants, Leon tossed the wallet in a nearby trash can and headed back onto the street.

Twenty minutes later, shod in stolen Nikes and carrying a backpack he'd bought from a homeless man, Leon set out to find something to eat and a place to hide. He had plans to make.

Chapter Eleven

Finding Grim wasn't easy. It took Leon nearly two days to score the items necessary to create a new identity for himself. Stolen clothes, a fake I.D., a haircut and some brunette dye, a pair of non-prescription hazel contacts to disguise his pale gray eyes. He even added a pair of horn-rimmed glasses with plain, slightly tinted lenses. After he was done, he barely recognized himself.

No one stopped him when he strode through the hospital's front door and began a wandering yet systematic search of the building. He didn't dare ask the elderly volunteer at the information desk for Graham Holmes' room, but instead kept his eyes peeled for the undercover operatives he knew damn well Jones had stationed near Grim.

He found them on the third floor, one in the Intensive Care waiting room, another pacing the hallway outside the ICU door. They were good. The general public never would've pegged them for what they were. But Leon knew. He'd been working for the organization long enough to recognize the cold, watchful eyes.

At the next regular visiting period, he managed to sneak into the ICU by insinuating himself into the midst of a crowd of anxious families. Grim's name wasn't posted outside the door of his room, but it was easy enough to guess which cubicle was his. The drawn curtains, the lack of visitors, and especially the woman sitting in a chair outside the little room, wearing what Leon knew was a fake police uniform and reading a magazine, gave it away.

Leon's heart hammered against his breastbone. He longed to yank back the curtains, run into the tiny room and see for himself that Grim was still alive and breathing. Instead, he put on his best lost visitor expression and approached a nurse writing on a chart across the room from Grim's cubicle. Maybe he couldn't see Grim right now, but he could sure as hell get the lay of the land without arousing suspicion.

"Excuse me," Leon addressed the nurse in a nasal voice slightly higher than his own.

The woman looked up and smiled. "Yes?"

"So sorry to disturb you, ah..." Leon squinted at her name tag. "Sherri, but I'm afraid I'm rather muddled. You see, I had thought my friend Michael was here in this ICU, but he doesn't seem to be."

"Maybe he's on another floor." Closing the chart, Sherri motioned Leon to follow her to the nurse's station. She sat down at a free computer and started tapping on the keyboard. "What's his last name?"

"Roberts. Michael Roberts."

Nodding, Sherri tapped the keys again. Hoping there would be enough Michael Roberts in the system to make the search take a minute, Leon surveyed the ICU. It was laid out in an L shape, with the nurse's station in the middle. The double doors leading inside were situated at the end of the shortest leg. Another set of doors were visible at the end of the long leg. Leon made a mental note to find out where they led.

"Hmm, well, there's a Michael Roberts on the fifth floor." Sherri glanced up at him. "When was your friend admitted, do you know?"

"Yesterday," Leon told her.

"Oh, then that's not him. Hang on."

While she searched through more Michael Roberts, Leon watched the visitors and staff come and go around him. The other set of double doors swung open, admitting a burly young man pushing a large covered cart. Leon caught a glimpse of what looked like another hallway beyond the door before it shut again.

"Okay," Sherri said. "There was a Michael Roberts admitted to the Adult Medicine unit yesterday. That's on this same floor, maybe that's how you got mixed up."

Leon beamed at her. "Yes, I'm certain that's it. Thank you, Sherri."

"My pleasure." Giving him a smile and a pat on the arm, she went back to her chart.

Leon glanced at the second doorway. He wanted to find out what lay beyond it. Knowledge was power, and he needed all the power he could get right now.

Plastering a vaguely puzzled look on his face, he wandered down the longer leg of the L and pushed open the double doors. He emerged in a bare, utilitarian hallway. To his left, about thirty feet away, were more double doors. A red sign over the doorway warned "Operating Room: Designated Personnel Only". Another set of doors directly in front of Leon were marked "Recovery". The right-hand leg of the hall took a sharp right turn a little ways down, with an elevator bank at the bend of the hallway.

The surgical suites and recovery room wouldn't be any help, so Leon walked down the hall to the right. Around the turn was another set of double doors. He shoved them open, and found himself back in the hall where he'd started.

"Well, that was pretty much useless," he muttered, pushing

the fake glasses up the bridge of his nose.

He glanced around. Staff and visitors hurried back and forth along the hall, none of them paying him any attention. Ducking back through the doorway, Leon summoned the elevator and pushed the button for the first floor. He needed to find a back way into the hospital if at all possible, and this looked promising.

The elevator doors opened on the second floor to let in a housekeeper pushing a laden cart. Leon saw another hall, bustling with activity, before the doors slid shut.

The short, round woman pinned him with a needle-sharp black gaze. "You lost?"

"Oh yes, I'm afraid so." Leon smiled at her, doing his best to look grateful instead of irritated. "Could you please direct me to the front entrance?"

"Sure." The doors opened on the first floor, and the woman pushed her cart out into yet another hall. Leon followed her, noting the maze of passages branching off from this one, leading to the pharmacy, the morgue, the laundry.

The housekeeper took one right turn followed by two left turns, and stopped at an intersection with another hall. "Follow this hall," she said, pointing to the right. "When you come to the doors, go on through and keep going straight. It leads right back to the front."

"Thank you so much." Leon gave her a little bow. "You've been most helpful."

With a curt nod, the woman turned around and went back the way she'd come. Leon waited until she'd gone, then strode down the left-hand leg of the hall, the opposite direction from what she'd indicated, following the sign to the loading dock. Loading docks were outside, which meant he may have just found his alternate way in.

Sure enough, the hall ended in a set of large automatic doors leading out to a covered concrete slab surrounded by trucks. A ramp descended to the parking area on the left, a set of steps on the right. On the other side of the parking lot was a two-lane road, and across from that a wooded park.

"Perfect," Leon whispered, eyeing the trees and shrubs. "Absolutely perfect."

He glanced around. Two men stood huddled against the side of a delivery truck a little ways off, smoking and talking. An ambulance sat parked a few dozen yards away at the emergency room entrance. Its red lights flashed against the dull brick of the hospital's outside wall. Staff and visitors strolled along the sidewalk between the parking lot and the road, or sat eating their lunch at the huddle of picnic tables in the small park.

Just enough people around that no one's going to pay any attention to one more.

Keeping his gait unhurried, Leon tucked his hands into his pockets and sauntered across the street to the park. A paved, flower-lined pathway wound off through the trees. Wooden benches sat at each curve of the path. There were no lights. At night, this park would be darker than the pit.

Oh yeah. Perfect.

Something rustled in the undergrowth ahead, just off a bend in the path. Leon heard a faint hiss of indrawn breath, followed by a groan so faint he wasn't certain he'd heard it. Moving silently, he crept up to the edge of the path and peered through the line of shrubs.

A few feet away, a young woman in pink scrubs sat huddled on a blanket on the ground. A lighter, a bent and blackened spoon, and a plastic bag with a film of white powder still clinging to the inside sat on the blanket beside her, along with other paraphernalia. As Leon watched, she injected the

149

last of the drug into her vein, pulled the needle out and stuck it in the ground. She snapped the tourniquet off her thin arm and rolled down the long sleeves of the black shirt she wore under her scrub top. Her expression was blissful as she rubbed the injection spot.

Leon could've whooped with delight. A hospital employee, mainlining at work. This skinny girl with the mousy ponytail and a dangerous addiction was about to become his information superhighway to everything Grim.

Blackmail and bribery were wonderful things.

The girl didn't even notice Leon's approach until he crouched on the ground beside her. She squeaked, hazy brown eyes blinking at him. "Who are you?"

"No one in particular." He smiled at her. "Good stuff?"

She narrowed her eyes at him. "You a cop?"

"God, no. Just a fellow slave to the poppy." He gestured toward the empty bag. "You're out, it looks like."

Her thin shoulders slumped. "Yeah. Can't get any more 'til the next payday."

"And when's that?"

"Almost two weeks. I had to pay rent this paycheck. There wasn't much left after that." She stared at him, hope blazing in her eyes. "Hey, you know where I can score some?"

"Sure," Leon lied. "I can bring you some, if you'll help me out with something."

She nodded, pathetically eager. "Yeah, yeah, anything you want. What is it?"

"I have a friend in the ICU. I'm afraid he's headed for prison once he's better." Leon sighed, arranging his face into a sad expression. "But the cops won't let me see him, and I really need to get a message to him."

The girl giggled. "No problem. I'm a phlebotomy tech—that means I draw blood for the lab—so I'm in the ICU all the time. I can give him a message, sure. Just tell me which room and all."

"That's great, uh..." He made a helpless gesture. "What's your name?"

"Tamara Rollins." She held out her hand, grinning a heroin-fueled grin. "Call me Tammy, everybody does."

Amused, he shook her hand. He could feel her delicate, bird-like bones through her skin. "My name's John. John Wallins. Nice to meet you, Tammy."

She retrieved her hand and stared up into the branches overhead, her face vacant. Leon kept quiet. His mind was going a mile a minute, trying to compose a message he could trust her to deliver. He didn't think he'd have much trouble finding a heroin dealer in the city. A few more stolen wallets should give him enough money to buy what he'd need to keep stringing Tammy along.

"Tammy," he said, when she seemed to be nodding off, "don't you need to go back to work?"

She shook her head. "Naw, I was off at three."

Fuck. He'd been hoping to get a message to Grim today.

Composing himself, Leon trailed his fingers down her arm. When she glanced at him in surprise, he let his mouth curve into a seductive smile. "Why don't we meet tomorrow, on your lunch break? I'll bring you the best smack in the city, and you come ready to deliver a message to my friend. Okay?"

She nodded. "My break's at eleven. Meet me right here, yeah?"

Her eyes wouldn't quite focus, but her body language said she was definitely interested in what Leon pretended to offer.

He suppressed a shudder. *Christ on a pogo stick, I wouldn't want* that *even if I was straight.*

"Tammy," Leon said, "you're a lifesaver. Thank you."

He kissed the back of her hand. Her skin tasted bitter, medicinal. She giggled, blushing, and he knew he had her.

Rising to his feet, he touched her flushed cheek. "Tomorrow, then. I'll look forward to it."

She stared up at him, looking dazed. "Yeah. Tomorrow. See you, John."

Smiling, he turned and made his way back to the path.

Before he reached the abandoned building where he'd taken up temporary residence, he'd stolen five wallets for a total score of three hundred dollars. Money in hand, he headed off to find a dealer.

ॐ

When he returned to the little park the next day, the heroin in his pocket, Tammy was already there.

"Hi," she called, waving at him. She took a bite of her sandwich and beckoned him over. "You got the junk?"

"Yeah. You ready to give my friend a message?"

She grinned. "I can do better than that. I'm supposed to be training a new employee, but he called in sick. You can pretend to be him, and I can get you into the ICU to see your friend."

Leon had to suppress a triumphant shout. This was far more than he'd expected. "That would be great. What do I do?"

Reaching into the plastic grocery bag lying on the ground beside her, she pulled out a pair of blue scrubs. "Put these on. I swiped the new guy's name tag out of his locker for you. Dumbass doesn't even have a lock on it. This scam won't work more than once, but just this one time no one'll notice. ICU nurses are too busy to pay any attention to one more lab tech."

Leon was impressed. If the girl hadn't been such a junkie, she might've been just the sort Jones' organization was always looking for. Acting on pure instinct, he grabbed her face in both hands and kissed her. "Tammy, you're an angel."

Her eyes took on a hungry gleam. "Yeah, well, this angel needs a fix."

"After I see my friend." Drawing back, Leon gave her a stern look. "This is important to me, Tammy. I need you to be clearheaded for this. Okay?"

She pouted, but didn't argue. "Okay. But you better have some damn awesome junk, yeah?"

"I do, Tammy." He kissed her again, dragging his tongue along her lower lip. "Trust me."

She didn't, he could tell, in spite of the way she trembled when he kissed her. But what choice did she have? It was either trust him, or go without her reason for living until payday.

He knew what she'd choose. Addiction was a bitch.

"All right," she whispered, her sour breath warm on his mouth. She clutched his shoulders with her thin fingers and pushed him away. "Go ahead and change. I gotta be back by eleven-thirty or I'm in trouble."

"Hmm, well, we wouldn't want that, would we?" Leon stood, letting his fingers trail down her neck as he pulled away. He toed off his sneakers and started stripping, making sure she got an eyeful of every muscled plane and curve of his body. "What do I do with my clothes?"

She licked her lips, brown eyes burning. "Just put 'em in the bag. You can hide them behind a tree or something. Nobody ever goes off the path here."

"You do," he pointed out, pulling on the scrub pants.

Her smile was bitter this time. "Yeah, well, not many other smack junkies in this place."

For a split second, Leon felt a pang of guilt. He shouldn't be using this girl's addiction against her. Feeding it, enabling it. It was wrong.

The feeling was a new one for Leon, and in the end it wasn't strong enough to overcome his current goal in life—getting Grim the fuck out of this place before Jones sent him to prison.

Promising himself he'd get Tammy to seek help as soon as he was done with her, Leon tugged the scrub shirt on, stuffed his clothes into the plastic bag and stashed it under a nearby bush. The bag would be invisible from the path. The smack should be safe enough. As an afterthought, he took off the horn-rimmed glasses and placed them in the bag with his clothes. It should be enough to keep anyone in the ICU from recognizing him.

"Okay, I'm ready," he declared. "Let's do this."

Tammy stood, rose up on tiptoe and kissed his chin. "Just do what I say, and you'll be fine. Now, who's your friend?"

"Graham Holmes. Room six in the ICU."

She nodded. "Okay. Let's go."

Leon trailed behind her, smiling to himself. *I'm coming, Grim.*

Chapter Twelve

To Leon's relief, Nurse Sherri wasn't there when he and Tammy entered the ICU. He trailed behind Tammy, trying to make himself look as calm and casual as possible while his skin crawled with tension and his heart kept trying to jump up his throat.

A tall, good-looking man with black hair and mocha skin grabbed Tammy's arm as they passed the desk. "Hey, are you drawing the CBC on six?"

"Yeah," she confirmed, shooting a swift glance at Leon.

"Good." He tapped the open chart sitting on the counter. "Dr. Schneider just added lytes to the noon labs."

"Got it."

"Cool, thanks." With a smile that probably had half the female staff swooning, the nurse patted Tammy's shoulder and hurried into a cubicle where several machines were screaming at once.

"What are those things?" Leon muttered as Tammy pulled identification stickers from Grim's chart and slapped them on three different collection tubes. "CBC and lytes, what are those?" He felt ridiculous asking, but after nearly four days away from Grim, with no idea what was happening, he was hungry for any information he could get.

"Complete blood count and electrolytes. Probably the most common lab draws for trauma patients." Tammy glanced around the ICU, then leaned closer. "When we go in, I'm gonna ask you to check his wristband. You can give him a quick message then, if he's awake enough to hear it."

Leon nodded. "Got it. Let's go."

The muscled hulk of a man in an ill-fitting police uniform who sat outside Grim's room didn't even look up from his Tom Clancy novel as Leon and Tammy approached. Leon was grateful, but it made him think less of Jones and the organization. A guard should question every person who approached their charge.

Maybe the local cops aren't normally that suspicious. Maybe that's why he seems like he's not paying attention, because he needs the staff to think he's local police.

Leon decided to believe that version. He couldn't afford to get sloppy now.

As he and Tammy entered the room, Leon's gaze zeroed in on Grim, and his breath huffed out as if he'd been punched in the gut. Grim lay motionless under a thin sheet, his feet nearly hanging off the end of the mattress. Bluish shadows smudged the skin below his closed eyes, forming a sharp contrast with his bone-white skin. His parted lips were pale and cracked. A thick plastic tube emerged from the left side of his naked chest, coiling on the mattress beside him and snaking down the side of the bed to connect to a large plastic container. Another tube emerged from beneath the sheet, draining urine into a bag hooked to the bedframe. More tubes snaked into him from the machines huddled around his bed, feeding into two different veins in his arm. There was even a tube in his nose, connected to a machine pumping thick tan fluid into him.

The urge to grab Grim and run, just pull out all those

fucking tubes and get him the hell out of here, was strong. He resisted it by reminding himself that such a rash action might very well kill Grim. But damn, it hurt seeing Grim like this.

Tammy's slender hand clamped onto Leon's wrist as they approached the bed. "Keep it together," she hissed. "It looks awful, yeah, but it isn't, not really."

"What is all this shit?" Leon whispered, not even caring anymore if he sounded stupid.

"The chest tube's keeping his lung expanded," she explained, setting the carrier with her supplies in it on the bedside table and pulling a pair of latex gloves from her scrub pockets. "The catheter's draining his bladder. The IVs are for fluids and meds, and the one in his nose is for tube feedings." She frowned. "You better not spazz out and get me in trouble."

"I won't." Leon drew a deep breath, willing himself to stay calm for Grim's sake. "I'm fine."

She didn't look entirely convinced, but she nodded. "Okay, Darren," she said, raising her voice to address Leon by the name on the borrowed tag. "Before we draw blood, we always have to check the patient's I.D. bracelet. You go ahead and do that, yeah? Make sure this is Graham Holmes. I'll be getting the tubes and stuff ready."

Leon edged past Tammy to stay by the head of Grim's bed. His heart pounded so hard it hurt. Taking Grim's limp hand in his, he bent low as if to peer at the white bracelet around the thin wrist.

"Grim," he murmured, as loudly as he dared. "Wake up. It's me."

Grim's brow furrowed. His eyes opened. They were hazy and unfocused. "Leon?" His voice was a rough whisper, thankfully too soft for Tammy to hear. He swallowed, wincing as if it hurt. "They're gonna send me to prison."

Leon smiled, fighting off the need to wrap Grim in his arms and just hold him. "Not if I can help it. Listen, there's not much time, but I'm getting you out of here. Soon as you're well enough, I'll be back. Okay?"

A faint smile curved Grim's lips. He didn't speak, but turned his wrist in Leon's grip and slid his hand down. As his long fingers wove through Leon's, his gaze sharpened and focused, piercing Leon like a rapier. It only lasted a second before Grim's eyes hazed again, his hand going slack in Leon's, but that one perfect second was enough to sustain Leon for days on end.

Leon squeezed Grim's fingers before letting go and moving away so Tammy could draw the blood for the lab work. He stood there, nodding and smiling while Tammy pretended to explain the process to him. Her voice was a meaningless drone in his ears. All he could think of was Grim, and the trust in those brown eyes. The past several days, he hadn't even been able to admit his greatest fear—that Grim would've lost whatever belief he'd had in Leon after the debacle at the cabin. That he'd never open his heart and soul to Leon again, the way he had the night before Jones' people found them.

Maybe there was hope after all. Leon had to believe there was. Otherwise, what point was there in anything?

Tammy tugged on his sleeve, bringing him out of his thoughts. "Okay, Darren, c'mon. We have another draw in the ICU then we'll send these to the lab. I'll show you what to do."

Nodding, Leon followed her out of the room. He risked a swift glance back through the glass door as they left. Grim's eyes had drifted closed again. His sleep seemed more peaceful than it had before, and Leon wondered if it was due to his visit, or if he was imagining things.

Leon decided the change was real, and had happened

because of him. There was no harm in believing it, even if it wasn't true.

℘

An hour later, Tammy got out of work early by way of a fairly convincing display of fake illness. Leon figured her addiction probably went a long way toward making her story believable. She looked terrible, her face pasty and slick with perspiration and her hands shaking. He held onto her elbow, pretending solicitous concern as they walked out of the hospital together.

She was pulling a zippered bag with pictures of kittens on it out of her purse before they even reached the clearing. "Where's the junk? I need a fix real bad."

"I'll say." Shaking his head, Leon retrieved his clothes from under the bush, fished the little bag of heroin out of his pants pocket and tossed it to her. "There's more where that came from, if you can keep me supplied with information."

"Yeah, sure." She pulled a small towel out of her purse and spread it out on the ground. "What d'you need to know?"

"I want daily updates on his condition. When he gets all those fucking tubes out of him, I want to know. When he's able to get out of bed and walk more than a few feet, I need to know about it. When they move him out of the ICU into a regular room, I need to know when and where. And I need to know as soon as they think about releasing him."

"You got it." She gave him a curious look. "Why the hell didn't you just tell me you were fucking him? I still would've helped you."

Leon closed his eyes and counted to ten in his head. When

he opened his eyes again, Tammy was already cooking the drug in the spoon. "I didn't tell you because it's none of your fucking business."

"Whatever." Her trembling thumb lost its grip on the lighter's wheel, snuffing out the flame. Grimacing, she relit it. "Meet me back here tomorrow at three-thirty. I'll give you an update."

With a curt nod, Leon turned on his heel and marched back to the path, not even bothering to change out of the stolen scrubs. His thoughts were already turning to the next stage of the plan.

He had a contact in Canada. Melissa, last name unknown. She owed him one for saving her skin five years ago when they'd been on a rare two-person job together. She was smart, and too slippery for even Jones to catch.

Striding down the sidewalk to the main road, Leon dug through his brain until he found Melissa's private number. He hoped it still worked. If she couldn't help Leon and Grim disappear, give them the chance to live together in peace, no one could.

Ꙭ

Nine days passed. Leon counted them, marking off each sunrise with a pen stroke on the wall of the empty building he'd chosen for shelter. The days were growing shorter and cooler. On the third evening, Leon was obliged to steal warmer clothes and a couple of blankets. While he was at it, he decided to get clothes for Grim as well. Jeans, underwear and socks, a thick sweater, gloves and a knit cap, and a pair of sneakers he was pretty sure would fit. He hoped it would do until they could get out of the city.

Grim moved out of ICU on the sixth day. According to Tammy, all the tubes were out and he was much more alert. Best of all, he'd begun walking a little. No farther than a few feet down the hall from his room, so far, but Tammy assured Leon that would change quickly.

"The doctor's note today said they're thinking about letting him go in the next couple of days," Tammy said on the ninth afternoon, teeth chattering in the icy breeze moaning through the trees of the park. They stood at the head of the path this time, just inside the tree line. She hugged herself and scowled up at the low-hanging clouds. "Graham says to tell you he's ready when you are. Whatever *that* means."

Leon shoved his hands into his jacket pockets and stared across the street at the hospital. "Is he still guarded?"

"Yeah. I've seen two different guys, working in shifts." She sucked on her bottom lip, her expression unusually thoughtful. "I don't think they're real cops."

"What makes you say so?" Leon kept his face impassive. There was no reason for Tammy to know the truth of the matter.

"I've seen cops guarding patients before. These guys just seem different. You can feel 'em watching you." She shrugged. "I don't know. Maybe I'm imagining things."

"Yeah, probably."

Leon walked over and sat on one of the wooden benches. His brain was racing. Jones had to know he would try to spring Grim. But she'd expect him to be watching the hospital, to try and free Grim on the transfer. She couldn't know about Tammy. That gave Leon an edge.

He had to get Grim out as soon as possible. Tonight, if he could manage it.

Tilting his head back, he gazed up into the heavy gray sky.

He desperately wanted to let Grim know he was coming for him, but he couldn't think of a way to do it without arousing suspicion. *Fuck.*

He stood, pulled the small plastic bag out of his pocket and pressed it into Tammy's hand. She'd already used up the first bag he'd bought her. "Here. It's brown this time. Couldn't get hold of the same dealer as before."

"Hey, you won't hear me bitching about it. This past week and a half would've been pure hell if it hadn't been for you." She closed her fingers over the bag. "I'm getting out of here before it starts raining. Same time tomorrow?"

He smiled. "Sure." They wouldn't be seeing each other again, but he couldn't tell her that. She'd hear all about Grim's escape on the local news anyway, and she was smart enough to put two and two together.

She stuffed the heroin into her purse and hurried down the sidewalk, giving him a little wave over her shoulder as she left. Leon watched her go. He waited until she'd turned the corner out of sight before mouthing, *Thank you.*

♋

At eight o'clock that night, Leon strolled through the front doors of the hospital with a large messenger bag slung over his shoulder and Stone Face's Glock in a shoulder holster beneath his jacket. He didn't even glance at the sign beside the door forbidding concealed weapons. He was just glad this hospital didn't have metal detectors.

Thanks to Tammy, he already knew what room Grim was in. He slouched past the information desk, unmanned at this hour, and headed for the visitor's elevators. The two security guards leaning against the wall talking didn't even glance his way.

He rehearsed the getaway plan in his head as the elevator carried him up to the fifth floor. According to the hospital map Tammy had procured for him, Grim's room wasn't far from a back stairwell. After turning the problem over and over in his head, Leon had decided not to take Grim out by the elevator. They would have to pass the nurses' station, destroying any hope of getting away without being seen. They would have to take the stairs to the first floor, then leave through the loading dock entrance. If they were spotted leaving Grim's room, they could exit on the third floor and head for the staff elevator he'd found on the first day.

If none of it worked, there was always the gun. Leon wasn't above threatening a few innocents if he had to. Anyone who forced him to shoot them wasn't innocent anyhow.

The elevator doors opened with a soft *ping*. Leon stepped out and followed the signs to Trauma Care. Before reaching the nurse's station, he pulled a stolen PDA out of his jacket pocket and flipped it open. He kept his head bent over the device as he strode past the desk.

A couple of other visitors strolled down the hall, and a petite woman in a surgical cap and rumpled scrubs stood writing on a chart outside one of the rooms. Leon smiled to himself. This was perfect—enough other people around that one more wouldn't seem suspicious, yet not so crowded that there was no chance of sneaking away unseen.

He stopped just outside room five-thirteen and put the PDA back in his pocket. His heart hammered so hard he could hear the rush of blood in his ears.

Get a grip, asshole. Grim needs you. Do not fuck this up.

Leon glanced around. The room was situated in the middle

of a short stretch of hall on one end of the rectangular nursing unit. A desk with a computer and phone sat against the wall behind him. The room to the left of Grim's was empty. The one to the right had the door shut tight, and Leon could hear a TV turned up far too loud. There was no one around.

It was now or never. Leon drew the pistol, thumbed off the safety and flung the door open in one movement.

A tall, hulking man was rising from a chair in the corner, gun lifting to aim as Leon kicked the door shut. Leon fired three rounds directly into the man's chest, the suppressor muffling the shots to a barely audible *thunk-thunk-thunk*. The guard crumpled to the floor.

Grim was already sitting on the edge of the bed, pulling the IV needle out of his arm. One wrist was cuffed to the bedframe. "The guard's got the keys," he said, indicating the cuffs.

Nodding, Leon squatted on the floor and began searching the guard one-handed. He kept his weapon trained on the closed door, just in case. The keys were hanging half out of the guard's pants pocket. Leon grabbed them. He took the man's gun as well and stuffed it into his bag.

Grim held out his hand. Leon laid the keys in his palm. "How long before the nurses are likely to come in?" Leon asked, keeping one eye on the door while Grim freed himself.

"She was just here a few minutes ago." Grim pressed a corner of the sheet to the bleeding puncture in his arm, where his IV had been. "She won't be back for another couple of hours."

"Good." Leon opened the messenger bag and pulled out the clothes and shoes he'd brought. "Put these on. We're going down the back stairs."

Grim nodded. "What do we do once we're out of the hospital?"

"I have a friend who owes me a favor. She's meeting us at the harbor and taking us by skiff to her private yacht. We just have to make it to the water."

The news, not to mention Leon's murder of the guard, was met with stoic acceptance on Grim's part. That cold practicality in the face of something which would've had most people half-catatonic with terror was what finally convinced Leon that this wasn't all some awful mistake. Only someone who had killed before could watch a person get shot to death right in front of him without any hint of emotion.

It was a relief, in a way. At least Leon wouldn't have to worry about Grim panicking or hesitating. He'd do what needed doing, and worry about the consequences later. But Leon still wished it didn't have to be this way. That Grim could've had a normal life, untouched by death and perversion.

Of course, the very tragedies Leon wished he could erase from Grim's past were part of what had shaped the person Leon had fallen helplessly in love with. So what, exactly, would he change, if he could?

He didn't want to think about that. Certainly not now. Maybe not ever.

Leon positioned himself at the door, pistol pointed at the ceiling, while Grim dressed. Grim's movements were stiff, his brow creased with pain, but he was clothed within a couple of minutes.

"Ready?" Leon asked as Grim crossed the room to stand beside him.

"Yeah." Grim held out his hand. "Give me the other gun."

Leon stared. "What?"

"I want the guard's gun." Grim paled and bit his lip. "Umm, please?"

Oh Christ, not now. "Grim, I'm not your fucking master. You don't have to...to be that way. I just don't think you should be armed right now. No offense, but I don't know how well you handle a gun, or how willing you are to pull the trigger if you need to."

Grim lifted his chin. "I killed someone, Leon. You do it once, it just makes it easier to do it again. But I bet you already knew that."

Leon's lips curled into a humorless smile. He'd never told Grim about his past line of work, but Grim was a smart kid. It didn't take a genius to realize Leon was no stranger to killing, given what he'd just done.

He searched Grim's face, seeking reassurance that he wouldn't get them both killed if he was armed. His cheeks were still blanched with the fear of standing up to Leon, but his dark eyes didn't flinch, and his hand was steady.

Reaching into his bag, Leon pulled out the guard's gun and handed it to Grim. "Neither of us is shooting anyone else unless we have to. Agreed?"

"Yeah." Grim checked the safety, then popped the magazine out. It was full. He slapped it back in and drew back the slide. There was a round already chambered, which didn't surprise Leon at all. Grim shoved the pistol into the front pocket of his jeans, and let the long sweater fall down to cover it. "Let's go."

Holstering his Glock, Leon cracked the door open and peered through. A nurse hurried past and disappeared around the corner. No one else was in sight.

"Clear, for now." Leon opened the door and motioned Grim through.

They moved together to the corner where the stairwell door was located. A man and woman were walking away from them along the other leg of the hallway. Neither of the two turned around as Leon eased the door open and he and Grim started down the stairs.

"We're heading to the first floor," Leon explained. "This stairwell exits on a side hall. We turn left onto that hall, then left again, straight through the double doors and out the loading dock entrance."

"Got it."

Leon gave Grim a sharp look. "You sound out of breath. You okay?"

Grim nodded as they rounded the first landing and clattered down to the next one, where a door led to the fourth floor. "It still sort of hurts to breathe, but it's not so bad."

Leon touched Grim's cheek. "You have to tell me if you think you won't be able to keep up the pace. This is no good if you wear yourself out before we even get out of the building."

"I know." Grim turned and planted a swift kiss on Leon's palm. "I'll tell you, I promise. Right now I'm fine."

The sweat beading on Grim's brow and the faint gasp in his voice said differently, but Leon didn't argue. There wasn't time to second-guess each other.

I'll carry him if I have to. There's no way I'm letting him go to prison.

They made it to the first floor without incident. Grim was breathing hard, his face lined with pain and effort. As they left the stairwell and started down the hall to the loading dock, Leon shot a concerned look at his companion. Grim gave him a faint nod and a smile, which didn't alleviate his worry in the least. He wished he could slide an arm around Grim's waist and help him along, but he didn't dare. There were too many people around. None of them were currently paying Leon and Grim the least bit of attention, and Leon didn't want that to change. The more invisible they were, the better. Walking arm-in-arm would draw unwanted and possibly dangerous attention.

When the loading dock doors slid open and they emerged into the biting cold of the early October night, Leon felt a hundred pounds lighter. Not that they were out of danger just yet. Not by a long stretch. But the touchiest part was behind them. If they could just keep their guard up a little while longer, they'd be on Melissa's yacht and headed for Canada. Melissa already had fake passports and I.D.s made up for them. Safety and blissful anonymity were so close Leon could taste it.

"The bus stop is just down the street," Leon murmured, taking Grim's arm. "Even if they've found the guard by now, we should be fine to take the bus to the docks. The nurses'll call the local police, and of course the Juneau police department doesn't even know about the organization. By the time Jones finds out, we'll be long gone."

Grim frowned. "What's the organization? And who's Jones?"

Before Leon could speak, something hard was pressed to the small of his back, and a familiar, hated voice responded to Grim's question.

"That would be me, Mr. Holmes."

Chapter Thirteen

Leon let go of Grim's arm and raised his empty hands into the air without being told. "Jones. Where the fuck did you come from?"

"Really, Mr. Fisher, you're becoming unforgivably careless if you think having a drug addict run messages for you won't arouse suspicion. True, it took longer than it should have for my people to notice, but eventually they did. Today, if you want to know." She huffed. "I was most disappointed with their ineptitude. They will be properly chastised, I assure you."

Fuck. Should've been more careful, Fisher, you fucking asshole. "And how'd you know I'd move tonight?"

"Luck, if you will. Mr. Holmes' guard overheard him telling your informant earlier today that he was ready. The guard deduced the rest. One of my men paid a visit to the girl today at her home. She was most talkative, once he threatened to turn her in to the local police. She seemed to believe you would be in to visit your young lover this evening. So I waited for you."

"Why?" Leon itched to whip around and snap her neck, but it would be suicide and he knew it. *Patience. Wait for your chance.*

Jones' hand slipped under his jacket and withdrew his gun. "You were the best, once. I'd hoped you could be the best again. I'd hoped you would come back to us. Your escape dashed those hopes, but we couldn't very well leave you out there skulking around, now could we?" The barrel of Jones' gun left Leon's back. "Walk toward the park, please. Mr. Holmes, lace your fingers behind your back and walk beside him."

Grim did as he was told. The three of them started across the parking lot. Catching Leon's eye, Grim cut a swift glance down to the gun hidden under his sweater. The gun Jones didn't know Grim had, because she hadn't bothered to search him.

The look which passed between Leon and Grim was brief and silent, but Leon knew what Grim was thinking. Jones, for whatever reason, was alone. They couldn't expect that to last. The second they hit the shelter of the trees, they had to move. And Grim had the only undetected weapon.

Leon hoped to God Grim knew what he was doing. Otherwise, they might both be dead in a few minutes.

"What are you going to do with us?" Leon asked, mostly to keep Jones talking. He had a feeling he already knew the answer.

"Unfortunately, you and Mr. Holmes will both have to be eliminated. It wouldn't have been that way if you'd just consented to return to the organization, Mr. Fisher. Your young man here would have been turned in to the local authorities the day he arrived at the hospital, and you would have been back on assignment. I hope you realize you're responsible for your lover's death. Oh, but you already know what that feels like, don't you?"

It was all Leon could do to stop himself from turning and lunging at the fucking bitch. The fact that she knew how deep those words would cut was the only thing that stopped him. She knew how guilt had nearly destroyed him after Ted's death, when he'd believed Ted would still be alive if he'd been there to protect him. She wanted him to lose control, and there was no way he'd give her the satisfaction.

"What, you people couldn't find me without staking out the fucking hospital?" he growled. "You had to use him for bait? That's pathetic."

Jones said nothing, but Leon could feel the anger in her silence. He was right, and it struck a nerve with her.

Good. Anger meant carelessness. He and Grim could use that edge right now.

"An hour ago, I regretted that I would be forced to kill you," Jones said as they entered the park. "Now, I rather think I've changed my mind."

Adrenaline sang through Leon's body. *Now. It's got to be now.*

As if reading Leon's mind, Grim crumpled forward with a keening cry. "No! Don't kill us! Please! I don't want to die!"

His plaintive plea rang through the night air. It was a fantastic bit of acting. Leon didn't take the time to turn and see if Jones had reacted. He whirled, aiming a roundhouse kick at Jones' midsection. His booted foot caught her right in the stomach. She staggered backward with a grunt.

Grim had the pistol out of his pocket and trained on Jones' head before she could recover. "On the ground," he ordered. "Face down, hands laced behind your head. And drop the gun."

Her hand opened, the pistol thudding to the grass. The dappled glow from the streetlights outside the park winked against the metal. She raised a cool eyebrow as she lowered herself to the ground and assumed the position. "Be careful, Mr. Holmes. You are already wanted for one murder."

Grim's smile was cold. "Don't worry about me. I won't go to prison."

She laughed. "You're that confident in Mr. Fisher, are you?"

"Yes. But I'd do anything to keep from going there. Anything."

Leon had no idea if Jones caught Grim's meaning or not, but he did, and it sent an icy chill trickling down his spine. He understood why Grim would rather die than go to prison, given his background, but that didn't make it any easier to hear him say it even in veiled terms.

He glanced at Grim. "Keep her covered."

Grim nodded. "Got it."

Making sure he stayed out of Jones' reach and out of Grim's line of fire, Leon picked up Jones' gun. He planted one knee in the middle of her back, dug the muzzle of her pistol into the back of her skull, and fished his Glock out of her jacket.

"I don't guess you have my Wilson," Leon grumbled. He hadn't missed his custom-made pistol in weeks, but damn, he missed it now.

"Would I tell you if I did?"

Leon didn't even try not to smirk at the breathlessness in Jones' voice. "Fuck you, Jones."

"What now?" Grim asked.

Leon glanced up. Grim's aim was steady, but his chest hitched in rapid, obviously pained breaths, and Leon knew he couldn't keep his stance for long.

"We restrain her and leave her here."

He had no intention of doing any such thing, of course. She'd overheard his and Grim's escape plans. He couldn't leave her alive. He wasn't about to tell her that, though. If she knew he planned to kill her, she'd draw the extra weapon he was certain she had on her someplace and start shooting. Cuff her first. Make her think he was really going to let her live. *Then* shoot her.

Rising to his feet, Leon holstered his Glock. He kept Jones' .38 trained on her head. "She'll have cuffs on her someplace. Find them. I've got her covered."

Grim lowered his gun, relief clear on his face. He set the weapon on the ground—well out of Jones' reach, Leon noticed with approval—knelt beside her and started searching through her jacket. His technique was clumsy, as if he'd never searched a prisoner before. Which he probably hadn't, Leon realized.

When Grim put a knee between Jones' parted legs to stabilize himself, Leon knew instantly what she was about to do. He didn't have time for anything but a warning shout before she struck.

Her thighs clamped onto Grim's leg. She rolled, sending him sprawling sideways onto the ground. The shot Leon fired hit her shoulder. It didn't even slow her down. His second shot hit her upper arm when she lunged for Grim and dragged him across her chest. When her other hand came up, there was a Black Widow in it. She shoved the small but lethal gun into Grim's throat.

"Drop your weapon, Fisher," she panted, eyes gleaming madly. "Or I'll blow his carotid artery right out of his neck."

Leon almost did what she said. The look in Grim's eyes stopped him. A look that begged for death before confinement.

I won't let him die. I won't.

He held Jones' gaze and shook his head. "No."

Her mouth contorted into a rictus he assumed was supposed to be a smile. "You think you're good enough to take me out before I can kill him. You're wrong."

Knowing she wouldn't be swayed by words, he fired. The bullet dug a black hole right between her eyes. She went limp, her head falling back with a wet splat. The gun dropped from her fingers.

"Still the best," he whispered.

Grim disentangled himself from Jones' lifeless grip and stumbled to his feet. "Leon. Fuck."

Thumbing on the .38's safety, Leon went to Grim and pulled him into his arms. Grim clung to him, shaking. "I would've rather died, Leon. I would."

"I know." Leon drew back, staring into Grim's eyes. "But I wasn't going to let you die, and I wasn't going to let her take you away. I'd die myself first."

Judging by the way Grim's eyes widened, he understood what Leon was saying, but he didn't comment. Leon was grateful for that. This wasn't the best time to confess his feelings for Grim, even if he'd been ready, which he wasn't.

"We need to go," Leon said when the silence began to feel too charged. "You get her Black Widow. I'll carry the other guns in my bag."

"Okay." Grim pulled away and knelt to recover Jones' miniature gun. He grimaced, holding a hand to his chest. "God. Hurts."

After stashing the two extra pistols in his bag, Leon dragged Jones' body off the path and under a sprawling shrub. She'd be found probably within a few hours, but there was no point in making it happen faster by leaving her corpse in the middle of the path. He hurried back to Grim's side and slipped an arm around his waist, leaving enough distance between them for him to draw the Glock if he needed to. "Lean on me. We're going to have to find a car to steal."

"Thought we were taking the bus."

Leon frowned at the tightness in Grim's voice. "That was

before I knew she'd figured out I was coming for you. She'll probably have people watching public transport, just in case. I'm thinking she'll have expected that if we got out without her seeing us, we'd take a cab or bus to the outskirts of the city, hide out in the forest for a while, then go over the border on foot."

"Which is why we're going by water, huh? Because the organization wouldn't expect it."

"Exactly. Can you make it to the street?"

Grim nodded. "Sure. Let's hurry, okay?"

"Yeah."

Leon wanted to say more, but he wasn't sure what. Keeping his left arm tucked around Grim and his right hand resting on the butt of the Glock in his shoulder holster, he led Grim out into the night.

℃

Not far from the hospital, Leon found an unlocked Nova illegally parked in front of a fire hydrant and hotwired it. The car took them to within half a mile of the dock before it ran out of gas. They walked the rest of the way.

By the time they rounded the corner of a huge warehouse and saw the lights of a hundred boats glinting on the water, Grim's face was chalk-white and dotted with cold sweat. His breath came in wheezing gasps.

Leon practically dragged Grim across the road, past a battered vessel reeking of fish and someone's private schooner lit up and jumping with drunken partygoers, to the slip where Melissa's skiff was docked. A tall, muscular woman with a blonde ponytail stepped off the boat and hurried toward them.

"Nice night for a party," she observed, watching Leon's face.

"I don't drink, myself," he said, using the answering code Melissa had given him. "My boy here's had a little much, though."

The woman gave him a curt nod. "We're set up to deal with it. Name's Lucy, by the way. Come on, I'll help you."

Positioning herself on Grim's other side, she hooked a sturdy arm around him. Together, she and Leon carried him onto the skiff. Grim's head hung down and his feet dragged. If it hadn't been for the nearly painful grip he had on Leon's shoulder, Leon would've thought he'd passed out.

"We're almost there," Leon murmured as he and Lucy settled Grim into one of the padded seats. "As soon as we get to the yacht, you're getting some pain meds and going straight to bed."

Grim smiled and squeezed Leon's hand.

Leon sat beside Grim, an arm around his shoulders, and Grim curled up against his side while Lucy unhitched the skiff and started the engine. The night air stung Leon's face with its rough, salty caress as the boat picked up speed.

Out in the channel, the skiff pulled up alongside Melissa's fifty-foot yacht, the *Dark Spirit*. Grim managed to climb the ladder to the deck, with Leon close behind urging him on with clumsy encouragements. Melissa stood beside the rail, her deceptively sweet smile beaming at him.

"Leon!" She gave him a swift one-armed hug. "Shit, it's great to see you. Sorry it had to be like this."

"Yeah, me too. Thanks for this, Melissa." Leon pulled Grim close, holding him up. Grim's head lolled against his shoulder. "Where can I take him? He shouldn't even be out of the hospital yet, never mind running around the fucking city on foot."

Melissa's smile faded. Stepping closer, she lifted Grim's chin and frowned. "Let's get you inside, kid. I brought a doctor with us. Figured you might need him."

"Thank you, ma'am," Grim whispered, his chest heaving against Leon's hand.

Melissa practically melted on the spot. "Oh my God, you're adorable." Patting his cheek, she turned toward Lucy, who'd just scaled the ladder behind Leon. "Babe, can you help Leon get the kid inside? I'm gonna go find Dr. Hunky."

Lucy glared after Melissa. "Bitch," she grumbled, resuming her former place at Grim's side. "Come on. It's not far."

Leon grinned but said nothing as he and Lucy hauled Grim into the forward cabin and eased him onto the bed. Melissa had always enjoyed teasing her lovers, both male and female, with her casual flirtations. Said lovers uniformly hated it, but were always too enthralled by her to leave. He'd spent a fair amount of time in Melissa's company in the past. Her behavior had been at one time part of the background of Leon's life. After the stress of the past week and a half, the ordinariness of it was a comfort.

Dr. Hunky—whose real name turned out to be Dr. Martin Hughes—arrived a matter of minutes later, with Melissa on his heels. True to the nickname with which Melissa had christened him, he was young and ridiculously good-looking, with dark, wavy hair, brilliant green eyes and a jaw that could cut glass. He looked more like a movie star than a doctor, but even Leon had to admit he seemed to know what he was doing. After helping Grim remove his blood-splattered sweater, he checked Grim's pulse and blood pressure, listened to his lungs and heart, and inspected the various wounds.

Leon was startled to learn that Grim had undergone surgery to remove the bullet, which had lodged against a rib instead of exiting his chest. Tammy had never mentioned that.

Does it matter? Would it have changed anything?

He knew it wouldn't have. In any case, Grim was here, alive and safe. They both were. And in a few days, they'd begin their new life, free of all the pain and mistakes of the past.

No matter how much Leon wanted to be angry with Tammy for ratting on him, he couldn't. Not when it seemed his life was finally going right.

By the time the doctor pronounced Grim stable and left him with a bottle of pain pills and a stern order to stay in bed until the next morning, Grim was already half asleep. Leon sat beside him, leaned down and gave him a gentle kiss.

"Go on to sleep," Leon said, laying a hand on Grim's cheek. "I'm gonna go catch up with Melissa for a little while."

"'Kay." Grim's eyelids fluttered closed. He cranked them up to half mast, one hand reaching for Leon's. "You're coming back, right? You'll stay with me?"

Leon's throat constricted. He nodded. "Yeah. I'm not leaving you ever again."

Grim smiled. Raising Leon's hand to his mouth, he kissed his knuckles. Grim's brown eyes drifted shut, his fingers going slack as he relaxed into the pillows, already sound asleep.

Leon stayed there for a moment, just looking at him. The memories locked behind that sweetly slumbering face were enough to destroy most people, but Grim was strong. So strong that Leon felt humbled by him. Maybe Leon had found him in time to keep the weight of experience from crushing him.

Maybe, just maybe, he could help make Grim whole again.

He's already done that for me.

A small hand gripped Leon's shoulder. "Hey, he needs to sleep. C'mon up on deck, we'll talk."

Leon looked up into Melissa's eyes. "Yeah. Okay." Leaning down, he laid a kiss on Grim's brow, tasting sweat and salt spray on the cool, pale skin. "Be back soon," he whispered.

He and Melissa left the cabin, closing the door quietly behind them, and walked up onto the deck. Away from the Juneau harbor, the night was pitch black and silent. The only sound was the susurration of the water against the bow of the boat.

"I'm sorry about Ted." Melissa leaned her elbows on the railing and stared out toward the barely visible shoreline. The breeze whipped her wavy red hair around her head. "I sent you a card, but I never knew if you got it."

"Yeah, I got it. Thanks." Leon laughed, the sound soft and bitter. "He liked you, you know. Said you were too sweet and pretty to be a professional killer."

She snorted. "Yeah, well, he only met me once."

"And you made your usual impression." He leaned on the rail beside her, studying the white foam streaking the water from the yacht's passage. "I killed Jones tonight. Shot her in the head."

"Good. I hated that fucking bitch." Melissa glanced at him. "They'll come after you for that."

"I know."

"Is he worth it?"

In his mind's eye, Leon saw Grim carving him a crutch, cleaning his wounds day after day, sharing his home and his food. Giving without ever asking anything in return.

"Yeah," Leon said, glad the darkness hid the emotion in his eyes. "He is."

Chapter Fourteen

The weather cleared as the yacht made its meandering way south down the Inside Passage and along the coast to Vancouver. Leon and Grim spent the bright October days on deck, talking. They spoke of little things at first. Safe things. Reminiscing about some of the fun times they'd shared at the cabin, planning what they'd do once they found a place to settle. It was nice, just spending time with Grim like this, and Leon felt years of tension melting away with every moment they sat side by side in the sunshine.

Twenty-four hours from the Vancouver harbor, Grim started the conversation they'd been working toward all along by asking point blank about Leon's background.

"I always knew you were dangerous," Grim said, picking at a splotch of paint on the leg of the borrowed jeans he wore. They sat on the deck, backs resting against the wall of the cabin behind them. "You just... I don't know. You seemed dangerous. Like you could really hurt me, if you wanted to." He stared at Leon, brown eyes serious. "I knew you wouldn't. I always knew that, even when I was scared of you."

"Good. I wondered sometimes." Taking Grim's hand, Leon wound their fingers together. "So, you want to know how I got to be so good at killing people, huh?"

Grim nodded. He watched Leon, his expression curious.

"I used to be an assassin," Leon told him, the words coming in a rush. "I worked for the government. At least I think I did. No one ever told me for sure, but I'm pretty sure that's who they were. Jones was the one who gave me my assignments, and my checks."

Grim nodded, rubbing his thumb along the back of Leon's hand. "Have you killed a lot of people?"

"Yeah. I don't know how many."

Scooting closer, Grim pressed against Leon's side. "Who was the last person you killed? Before now, I mean. Were you in Alaska to kill someone?"

Dread dug its needle claws into Leon's gut. His mouth went dry. Ever since he'd first made the decision to be with Grim, he'd known he'd have to tell Grim about Ted one day. He just hadn't expected it to happen so soon. He stared out over the water, trying to think of how to begin.

"Leon?" Grim's voice was soft, his grip on Leon's hand firm. "You don't have to tell me if you don't want."

You can do this, Fisher. He deserves to know everything.

"A little over a year ago," Leon began, watching the waves ripple and glint in the sun, "a man named Frank Gold tortured and murdered my lover, Ted. I hunted Gold down and killed him. I'd planned to torture him like he'd tortured Ted. But I looked at him, lying there tied up waiting for me to hurt him and telling me how Ted had screamed for me, and he was fucking *loving* telling me that, and all I could see right then was myself, because I knew it was gonna feel so fucking good to tear that fucker apart piece by piece. And I thought, what would make me any different from that fucking piece of shit Frank Gold, if I did the same thing to him that he did to Ted? Not a fair fight, not even a hunt-and-shoot, but carving up a man who can't defend himself."

"You couldn't do it." Grim's eyes searched Leon's, never wavering, and Leon was grateful for that. He didn't think he could stand to see fear—or worse, disgust—in Grim's face right now.

Leon nodded. "Right. I couldn't do it. In the end, I just shot him in the head and left. After that, I lost my edge. I couldn't focus, I couldn't do anything but drink every day until I passed out. All I could think of was Ted, and what happened to him, and how I'd gotten to be too much of a bad guy even for myself. Jones sent me to Alaska to get my shit together."

If any of Leon's revelations bothered Grim at all, he didn't show it. He simply nodded, scrunched down and laid his head on Leon's shoulder. "I guess it worked, kind of."

Leon laughed. "I guess so. Not the way she was thinking, but what the fuck. Right now, my life's better than it's been in a long time."

Grim tilted his head to smile up at Leon. "So's mine. Way better."

It was too perfect an opening to pass up. Sliding an arm around Grim's shoulders, Leon kissed his head. "What was it like, before?"

Grim tensed, but didn't move. "You mean with John?"

"Yeah. But not just with John. There's a whole lot more to you than whatever that fucking bastard did to you. Something made you join what's apparently a pretty notorious gang and end up killing a man. I want to know it all, when you're ready to tell me."

Grim said nothing. The silence stretched until Leon began to believe Grim wasn't going to answer. Not today, anyway. It was disappointing, but not the end of the world. When he was ready, Grim would tell Leon his story.

At least, Leon hoped he would.

182

After an endless few minutes, Grim sat up and pulled away from Leon's side. Leon watched with a frown as Grim drew his knees up to his chin and wrapped both arms around his legs.

"Grim, I know this must be hard for you." Leon felt clumsy and tongue-tied. He wished he could just say what he wanted to say. "I'm no good at this kind of shit, if it's too soon—"

"I ran away from home when I was nine," Grim began. His voice was flat, his expressionless gaze fixed on the horizon. "I don't think my parents even noticed when I left. I remember my mom was passed out on the floor. I don't even know what she was on. They were always high on something."

Leon forced back the string of abuse he was bursting to heap on Grim's parents. It wouldn't do any good now. He kept quiet and waited for Grim to go on.

"We lived in Anchorage," Grim continued after a moment. "After I left my parents' house, I lived on the street for a while. I stole wallets and food and stuff to survive. One time, I tried to lift this guy's wallet, and he caught me. He beat the crap out of me for it, but I put up a damn good fight." The corner of Grim's mouth lifted in a tiny smile. "Turns out he was high up in the Death Squad. He spoke up for me, and they let me join."

Leon studied Grim's profile. "Didn't your parents even look for you?"

Grim let out a short, bitter laugh. "I never went to school, because they never enrolled me, and I don't even know when my birthday is. What do you think?"

I think I'd like to kick their sorry asses.

Leon kept the thought to himself. He laid a hand on the curve of Grim's back, trying to convey his sympathy through touch. "Go on."

Grim's hand slid onto Leon's knee. "I was pretty much a messenger boy for the Death Squad. They were okay to me,

183

usually. Better than my parents anyway. At least I had food most days, and I learned how to look after myself. I got arrested a few times, for minor stuff. Went to juvie once. But mostly it wasn't so bad." He laughed, the sound sharp and without humor. "They're the ones who started calling me Grim. It was my gang name, the one nobody but them knew. They said it fit."

Moving closer, Leon hooked his fingers into the waistband of Grim's jeans. "What happened that night, Grim? When you shot that man." He hoped his bluntness didn't stop Grim from talking. Subtlety had never been one of his strong points.

Grim hung his head so that his hair hung over his face. "I was supposed to deliver the coke and get the money. That was it. This guy bought from us all the time, it was supposed to be easy. But he tried to rip us off. He took the coke, punched me in the face and ran. And I...I shot him. He didn't even know I had a gun, and I shot him in the back."

Something in Grim's voice said that moment still haunted his nightmares. Leon pulled Grim closer, following the overwhelming urge to comfort him. "You were fourteen. You panicked. It happens."

Grim's fingers tightened on Leon's knee. "I couldn't go back to the gang. They would've killed me, for losing the coke and not getting the money. So I ran."

"And John found you." *Fucking pedophile bastard.*

With a glance which suggested he knew exactly what Leon was thinking, Grim nodded. "I was hiding in the park. He saw me, and offered to help. I took him up on it."

For several minutes, they sat without speaking. Leon wound strands of Grim's silky hair between his fingers, trying to think of a way to ask all the questions whirling in his brain. He wasn't even sure why he wanted to hear the details of those years from Grim, when he'd already read the whole nauseating story in John's journal. If Grim was telling the truth, John was dead. Even if he wasn't, there was precious little Leon could do about it. Hearing Grim voice the things John had done couldn't accomplish a damn thing except make Leon angry, and make him hurt for Grim, and he hated feeling angry and hurt when he couldn't fix it.

But maybe talking about it would help Grim. He won't admit John abused him. Maybe talking's what he needs to do to face it and move on.

Leon almost laughed. He really was going soft if he was starting to think like that dumbass psychiatrist back in L.A.

For once, the idea didn't bother him.

"You said before that John saved you. That he took care of you." The words tasted vile on Leon's tongue, but he didn't let that show in his face. He wanted to get Grim talking about John, not alienate him. "Will you tell me about that?"

Grim hunched his shoulders. "He did, Leon. I know you don't believe me, but he really did. I'd have already been in prison for years now if it hadn't been for him."

The sincerity in Grim's voice made Leon's stomach clench with a mixture of sadness and fury. Technically, what Grim said was true. John *had* kept him out of prison. But manipulating a scared fourteen-year-old virgin into sex was, in Leon's opinion, no better than rape. At least in prison they didn't sugarcoat it.

"I read that journal," Leon reminded him. "I know exactly what he did."

Shaking his head, Grim covered his face with both hands. "What was he supposed to do? We were alone for almost six years. He needed sex, and I...I wanted it. I did. I'd just figured out I was gay, and he taught me all about how to get a man off. And, and of *course* he had to punish me when I did wrong. He didn't want to, he would always say he didn't want to do it, but

185

how else was I supposed to learn? I had to beg him, sometimes, he hated hurting me so much."

Leon shut his eyes and leaned his head against Grim's. He didn't feel angry anymore. The thought of John's creative and horrible punishments, all supposedly done "for the boy's own good", made him sick. He hated remembering the things he'd read in that fucking diary. He wished he could just bury his face in Grim's hair and let the scent of salt air and sunshine wash it all away.

If he could've gone back in time and somehow given Grim a chance for a normal life, he would've done it. He ached for the boy Grim had been, and even more for the profoundly damaged man he'd become. But he couldn't change the past. No one could.

All they had was the here and now. He and Grim would both just have to learn to work with it.

Wrapping both arms around Grim's shoulders, Leon kissed his temple. "Tell me, Grim. Talk to me. I promise I'll listen."

Grim didn't seem too sure of that at first—not that Leon could blame him, considering—but he talked, and Leon listened. It was hard hearing Grim justify the things John had done to him, but Leon shoved his anger at John savagely aside and held his tongue. Maybe saying it all out loud would force Grim to see it for what it was. Once he finally admitted how John had abused his body and his trust, maybe he could let John go.

Leon lost track of the hours as Grim told his story. It was eerie how closely the tone of Grim's tale matched that of the journal. It reminded Leon of the aftermath of his parents' frequent fights, once his father's whiskey-fueled rage subsided and his mother stopped sobbing on the floor. Abuser and victim each proclaiming the former's innocence in sickening stereo.

He'd hated it then, and he hated it worse now. But there was nothing he could do, except what he was already doing.

Listening.

As the afternoon faded into evening and the sinking sun set sea and sky on fire, something changed. The certainty began to ebb from Grim's voice. His eyes took on a startled expression, and Leon wondered if this was what it looked like when someone started to see the light at last.

During a particularly hair-raising tale of being tied naked to a tree like a dog and left there for a week, with no food and only enough water to keep him alive, Grim's words faltered. He turned to stare into Leon's eyes, his own wide and shocked.

"I let the rice burn," he said, repeating part of the story he'd just told. "I'd been working all day, fishing and cooking and cleaning and I was so tired. I hadn't slept much the night before because my...because I was sore. I was just going to rest for a minute while the rice cooked, but I fell asleep. John had been to pick up our supplies, and he got back and found me asleep and the rice was ruined, and..."

He trailed off. Leon brushed the hair from Grim's eyes and waited, wishing he could go back in time and rip John's heart right out of his rib cage.

After a moment, Grim shoved to his feet, stalked over to the railing and leaned against it. Leon followed, not knowing what to do. He felt awkward and out of his depth. Should he say something, or keep quiet? Would it be better to hold Grim, kiss him and stroke his hair, or keep his distance? He had no idea, so he went with his gut and simply rested his elbows on the railing beside Grim, close enough to reach out and touch him but far enough away to lend a sense of space.

"Why'd he do that?" Grim's voice was soft and small, his gaze fixed on the arc of blood-red light still visible where the water met the sky. "I didn't mean to fall asleep and ruin dinner. It was an accident. He said it was wrong, that if I wanted to sleep all day like a dog then I could live like one, and then I'd learn not to let those things happen. He kept saying it, over and over, and I knew he'd get mad if I didn't let him do it, so I said yes. I said I agreed, and I ought to be punished like a dog." He turned to look at Leon, the wind flailing his hair against his face. "But I didn't agree. I didn't think I deserved that."

Swallowing against the tightness in his throat, Leon shook his head. "No, you didn't. Nobody deserves to be treated that way, for any reason. Nobody. He was wrong, Grim."

Grim nodded, very slowly, his face white in the deepening gloom. "That time, he was. Yes."

It was a start. The rest would come, with time and patience. For Grim, Leon had plenty of both.

Chapter Fifteen

Five cars ahead, the light changed for the third time since Leon had become snarled in the afternoon traffic jam. Brow furrowed in determination, Leon rode the bumper of the battered orange van in front of him and managed to roll through the intersection just as the light turned yellow.

"Goddamn fucking festivals," Leon grumbled. He jerked his SUV into the right lane, cutting off a purple Beetle, and zoomed past the puttering van. "Why's everything have to happen at once in this fucking place?"

The complaint was more habit than anything. He and Grim had lived on the outskirts of Vancouver ever since they'd first arrived here ten months ago, and they'd both come to love the place. True, the current overlap of the Queer Film Festival and the annual string of summer concerts caused enough extra traffic to be aggravating, but Leon didn't really mind. He liked the eclectic mix of visitors it brought to the already vibrant and cosmopolitan city.

As he drove north, the traffic gradually thinned, and the skyscrapers gave way to neighborhoods where mothers talked across the hedges and kids peddled their bikes along the shaded streets. He turned down a narrow side road which wound away from the cozy homes and up into the hills, toward the private estate he and Grim shared.

As soon as he'd managed to transfer his considerable wealth to a Vancouver bank account under his new alias, Leon had gone looking for a real home to replace the apartment he and Grim had been living in for three weeks. After only a few days, he'd found twenty acres complete with a house north of the city and bought it for a mere twenty thousand from a rich widower with an urge to travel.

He'd kept the purchase a secret, wanting to surprise Grim with a beautiful place to call his own. Leon smiled, thinking of the moment Grim had first seen the sprawling cedar home. Grim had stood rooted to the spot for several minutes, wide-eyed and speechless, then calmly asked Leon if the place was really theirs. When Leon said yes, it was, Grim had nodded, flung himself into Leon's arms and pulled him to the ground. They'd made love right there in the thick, springy grass, heedless of the bite of fall in the air.

That still ranked as one of the finest moments of Leon's life.

Leon shook off the memories as he guided the SUV around the final curve in the drive and the house came into view, set in a green clearing among the tall pines. Sunlight glinted off the arched windows and threw bars of shadow across the lawn from the roughhewn beams supporting the deck.

It reminded him of the little cabin in the Tongass Forest. Not because of how it looked. This spacious, well-appointed home couldn't have been more different from the one-room shack hidden deep in the Alaskan wilderness. The common factor was the sense of belonging Leon had found in both places.

The cabin was the first place that had felt like home to Leon since Ted's death. This was the second. And the reason for that was waiting for him inside, probably already cooking.

Leon hit the button on the garage door opener's remote

control, pulled into the garage and shut the door again. Sliding out of the front seat, he opened the back door and grabbed the bags from his shopping trip. He'd probably gotten way too much. Grim would be scandalized by all the expensive things Leon had bought him. Hell, the kid would never get over how much Leon had paid for the champagne. But it wasn't every day a man celebrated his first anniversary, and Leon wanted it to be special.

Clomping up the stairs from the garage to the kitchen, with bags full of his various purchases hanging off both arms, Leon had to laugh at himself. *Check out the big, bad assassin now, huh?*

He didn't mind. In his opinion, he'd earned the quiet life, and so had Grim.

After a moment's wrestling with bags to get at the doorknob, Leon managed to get the door open and walked into the sunny kitchen. He kicked the door shut.

"Grim, I'm home," he called, setting his purchases on the floor long enough to retrieve the champagne from its specially made box. He drew a deep breath. The scent of beef and fresh vegetables roasting together made his mouth water. "Stay in the living room for a second, I need to put some stuff away."

No answer. Frowning, Leon deposited the champagne in the refrigerator and wandered into the living room, where he'd assumed Grim would be. "Grim? Where are you?"

The silence echoed in the vaulted ceiling. Apprehension clutched at Leon's insides. They'd disappeared from the face of the earth, as far as Leon's former employers were concerned. He was sure of it. There had been no sign that anyone had found them. Yet Grim was nowhere to be seen, when any other day he would've been in Leon's arms by now, making him forget all about food and presents and everything else.

The whole thing felt far too familiar.

Heart in his throat, Leon reached beneath his jacket and drew the new custom Wilson combat pistol he carried everywhere. He made a complete circuit of the downstairs rooms. Grim wasn't there.

Upstairs, all Grim's clothes were in place, all the books he'd bought once Leon started teaching him to read lay piled on the table beside the bed. Leon could even smell the scent of Grim's shampoo, and water still beaded on the shower curtain in their large, bright bathroom.

Leon hurried downstairs again, keeping his rage contained through sheer force of will. If they'd taken Grim, Leon would personally cut every motherfucking one of them to ribbons.

Storming past the sliding glass door leading to the deck, Leon caught sight of a long, pale leg hanging off one of the lounge chairs outside. He stopped, his pulse racing. It was definitely Grim's leg. He'd seen enough of Grim's body to know. There was no blood that he could see. It was a warm afternoon, maybe...

Leon wouldn't let himself finish the thought. Being wrong might break him.

Pistol at the ready, just in case, Leon eased the door open and sidled out onto the deck.

Grim lay stretched out on the chair, barefoot and shirtless. One hand held an open paperback face down on his chest. The other lay across his stomach, fingers loosely curled against the waist band of the godawful plaid shorts he loved to wear. He was sound asleep, and completely unharmed.

Relief swept through Leon. He blew out a breath he hadn't realized he'd been holding. Thumbing the safety on his pistol, he holstered it and perched on the edge of the chair beside Grim.

He removed the novel from Grim's slack hand and studied the cover. *The Flame and the Flower,* it read, in flowing script over a lush painting of a squared-jawed man in an open shirt and a buxom woman swooning in his arms.

Snickering, Leon dog-eared a page to mark Grim's place and set the book on the deck. Grim wasn't far enough along in his reading education to understand three quarters of the stuff he read, but he spent practically every waking moment trying. For reasons Leon couldn't fathom, Grim's favorite books were the old romance novels full of gruff but noble hero-type men and soft yet strong women having secret babies all over the place.

Leon didn't get it at all. He loved to watch Grim read, though, hunched over one of his lurid paperbacks, lips silently sounding out the words. It was adorable, not that Leon would ever say that out loud.

Leon brushed a hank of hair from Grim's face, leaned down and kissed his lips. "Grim. Wake up, baby."

Grim's nose scrunched. He stirred, yawning, and his eyelids fluttered open. For a second, he stared at Leon with a faintly puzzled expression. Then his eyes went wide and he sat straight up, clipping Leon's chin with his head.

"I'm sorry, John, I fell asleep, I didn't mean to." Grim's voice was high and panicked. "I'll fix it, I swear, I'm sorry."

He started to get up, shaking all over. Sighing, Leon wrapped his arms around Grim and held him still until the momentary confusion passed. It happened now and then when Grim woke from a deep sleep, his mind putting him back in his past with John. It never lasted more than a few seconds, but it broke Leon's heart to see the terror and despair in Grim's eyes.

The upside to the whole thing was, describing his nightmares and flashbacks to Leon had helped Grim see them for what they were—a result of years of physical, sexual and psychological abuse. He and Leon had both gotten better at talking honestly about their pasts, and it had brought them closer than Leon ever could have imagined. He couldn't help feeling smugly pleased that they'd come as far as they had without any sort of professional help.

After only a second's struggle, Grim relaxed in Leon's embrace. "I did it again," he said, his voice muffled in Leon's neck.

"Yeah, you did." Leon caressed Grim's bare back with both hands, loving the feel of the warm, slightly damp skin against his palms. "You okay?"

Grim nodded, his fingers gripping Leon's jacket. "I thought it was the time I fell asleep and burned the rice."

"I figured so." Thinking about that episode still made Leon see red. He drew back enough to look into Grim's eyes. "You want to talk about it?"

"Not right now. I don't even want to think about it." The shadow of past fear vanished from Grim's face, replaced by a sunny smile. "There's pot roast in the oven, and I made a key lime pie for dessert. I hope that's okay."

"Those happen to be two of my favorite things. But you know I'll eat whatever you make. You're a fantastic cook."

The blush which stained Grim's cheeks at the compliment made Leon want to kiss him, so he did. Grim's mouth opened under his, warm and wet and eager.

A less honest man would've said anything, whether it was true or not, for kisses like that. But for all Leon's past sins, he'd never been one to engage in idle flattery. Grim truly did have a rare talent in the kitchen.

As if in response to the thought of Grim's cooking, Leon's stomach gave a loud growl. Grim broke the kiss, laughing.

"Dinner should be ready soon. Let's go in, I'll fix you a salad or something while we wait."

Remembering the bags still sitting on the kitchen floor, Leon leapt to his feet, one hand on Grim's shoulder to keep him from getting up. "Stay there. I need to take care of a couple of things before you come in."

Grim's eyes narrowed. "Do these things you have to take care of have anything to do with you spending most of the afternoon in town shopping? And not letting me come with you?"

"Maybe." Leon grinned. "I bet you don't know what today is, because you didn't have a calendar or anything last summer, but I know."

Tilting his head sideways, Grim gave Leon a curious look. "What?"

Taking Grim's hand in his, Leon squeezed his fingers. "We first met a year ago today."

Grim's lips formed a silent "oh" of surprise. "It's our anniversary? Really?"

"Yeah, well, I might be a day or two off, but I think I got it right. Close enough, anyway." Leon ran a hand through the unruly curls Grim had begged him not to cut, trying to ignore the heat in his face. *God, you're crap with this romantic shit, Fisher.* "Anyhow, yeah, I, umm, I got some stuff to celebrate. I want to get everything set up before you come in."

Grim beamed up at him. "What all did you get?"

"It's a surprise." Leon lifted Grim's hand and kissed his fingers. "Now stay put, just for a few minutes."

Letting his hand slip from Leon's grip, Grim settled obediently into the lounge chair. His eyes sparkled. "I never had an anniversary before."

Which is why I want this one to be perfect.

Leon wanted to tell Grim how special he was. How he deserved far more than expensive gifts and fine champagne. But Leon knew if he tried to tell Grim how he felt, the words would come out all wrong.

I'll just have to show him, then.

No. You can't just show him how much he means to you. You have to tell *him too. You have to say it out loud.*

Bending, Leon lifted Grim's chin and brushed their lips together. "Stay. Relax. I'll be back."

Grim laughed. With one more lingering kiss, he let Leon go. Leon hurried back inside, smiling to himself. He had definite plans for the night. For once, his plans included words. Three of them, to go along with the gift he was saving for last.

No danger he'd ever faced had scared him as much.

ℂ

An hour later, Leon pushed away the remains of his second slice of pie and patted his stomach. "God, I'm stuffed. That was great, Grim."

"Thanks." Grim picked up the last bite of pie from his plate, popped it in his mouth and licked his fingers clean. "I like cooking. I always did, really, but it's a lot more fun when you have a real kitchen to work in."

"Yeah, I bet. Never could cook worth a damn myself." Shoving his chair back, Leon started gathering the dirty plates and silverware. "Why don't you go on upstairs? I'm gonna put away the leftovers and stick the dirty dishes in the dishwasher, I'll be right up."

Evidently his face wasn't as innocent as he'd hoped,

because Grim gave him a suspicious look. "What's going on? You already gave me a present." He held up the brand new video iPod Leon had bought him, and which he'd repeatedly reached out to stroke while they ate. "You spent all that time in here earlier and wouldn't let me come in, but the only thing down here was the iPod and the candles on the table. I know that didn't take long to set up. So what's upstairs?"

Shaking his head, Leon fished the plastic wrap out of the drawer and tore off a piece to cover the pie with. "The bed. I don't know about you, but I'm anxious to use it."

A lecherous grin spread over Grim's face. Jumping up, he stalked over to Leon and pressed a hard kiss to his mouth. "Hurry."

Leon watched, amused and more than a little turned on, as Grim whirled, ran to the stairs and bounded up them two at a time. Grim still needed a lot of encouragement to ask for what he wanted in bed, but his enthusiasm for sex was irresistible. Leon fully intended to make tonight all about Grim. His needs, his desires, his fantasies. Hopefully Leon's attempts at setting the proper mood would give Grim the courage to let himself go, and let Leon take care of him.

The absolute silence from upstairs could've been a good thing or a bad thing, but Leon was optimistic. Dishwasher loaded, leftovers wrapped and put away, Leon opened the fridge and took the champagne out of the bowl of ice water in which it had been chilling. He fetched the silver ice bucket and two crystal flutes he'd bought that afternoon, put the bottle in the bucket and surrounded it with ice from the freezer. With the silver pail tucked in the crook of one elbow and the flutes in his other hand, he started up the stairs.

When he walked into the bedroom, Leon had to choke back a laugh. Grim lay on his stomach on the bed, propped on his elbows, the box of Swiss chocolates Leon had set on the pillow open in front of him. A bit of cherry liqueur was smeared on the corner of his mouth. As Leon watched, he bit into what was clearly not his first of the candies.

"Oh, wow," Grim moaned. "These are soooo good."

His tongue darted out to lick a droplet of thick red liquid from his lip. Leon's cock jerked in response, remembering the feel of that soft, warm tongue on him.

"Glad you like them." Walking over to the bedside table, Leon set the pail and flutes down, picked up the box of matches and started lighting the candles he'd set on every available surface. "What do you think about the new bedclothes?"

"They're great." Grim flopped onto his back and spread his hands flat against the plush comforter. His pale skin glowed against the deep crimson fabric. "I love red."

"It looks good on you. Or maybe I should say, *you* look good on *it*." Leon flipped off the overhead light. The many candles cast a warm golden glow over the room. Crossing to the bed, Leon crawled onto the mattress and kissed Grim's flat belly. He drew a deep breath, catching a whiff of something fresh and green, like clover. Underneath that was the unmistakable tang of male arousal. "Mmm. You smell good."

Grim squeaked when Leon's tongue dug into his navel. "That tickles!" he protested, though the hands in Leon's hair seemed more inclined to hold him down than push him away. "Hey, you brought booze."

"Oh, so you noticed that finally." Grinning, Leon sat up and scooted to the edge of the bed. "It's not 'booze', you heathen. It's extremely expensive champagne."

A horrified expression crossed Grim's face. "Shit, Leon, you shouldn't have spent all this money. How much was that?"

"Don't worry about it. We can afford it."

"But, Leon, I don't d—"

"You better not say you don't deserve this," Leon interrupted, shooting a warning look at Grim. Plucking the bottle of Cristal out of the bucket, Leon wrapped a white hand towel around it and peeled the foil off the top. "You deserve all of this, and more."

Grim bit his lip, eyeing the bottle in Leon's hand as if it might come to life at any moment and chastise him for being greedy. "But if it really costs that much—"

"What have I told you about money?"

"That money's for spending, not keeping," Grim dutifully recited.

"And?"

"And you have a few million in the bank, and it's mine as much as it is yours, and I should never, ever, ever worry about spending too much because there's no such thing." Grim hunched his shoulders, watching with interest as Leon twisted off the wire holding the cork in place and began easing it out of the bottle. "Does it taste good?"

"Very. Your taste buds'll come like a fucking porn star, trust me." The cork came loose with a soft sigh. Picking up one of the flutes, Leon poured a bit in, waited for the foam to subside, then finished filling the glass. He handed it to Grim. "Here. Sip, don't guzzle."

Lifting the flute, Grim sniffed at it, then put the rim of the glass to his lips and took a cautious sip. The expression of bliss which came over his face was almost comical. "Oh, wow. You're right, that tastes amazing."

"Told you." Leon filled the other flute, settled cross-legged on the mattress beside Grim, and lifted his glass. "To us. To another year."

"To us," Grim echoed, eyes shining. They clinked glasses and drank.

"Mmm." Licking his lips, Grim took another, longer swallow. "I think I like champagne."

Leon laughed as Grim emptied his glass in a few gulps. "How would you know? You're not even stopping to taste it."

The smile Grim gave him made his cock twitch and start to swell. Rising to his knees, Grim leaned over, set the empty glass on the table and settled himself astride Leon's lap. "I guess I'll just have to taste yours instead," he said, winding both arms around Leon's neck. He dipped his head and licked the rim of the glass Leon still held. "C'mon, Leon. Let me taste yours."

Grim's voice was a seductive purr, but his eyes sparkled with mischief. Leon thought he'd never looked more desirable.

"Oh, I'll let you taste mine, all right." Leon slid one hand into Grim's hair, cupping the back of his head, and held the rim of the flute to his lips. "But first, have some of my champagne."

Grim snorted and nearly choked on his first sip. Getting himself under control, he drew some of the golden liquid between his lips and held it in his mouth for a moment before swallowing it. Leon stared, entranced by the way his Adam's apple moved under the smooth, pale skin of his throat.

The moan Grim let out was obscene. "Oh, God, that's good." He ground his crotch against Leon's belly. "All this booze and chocolate's making me horny. Can we fuck now?"

"Hell yeah, we can fuck now." Setting his glass aside, Leon reached between them and rubbed Grim's erection through his shorts. "You're so fucking hot. You make me want you all the time."

A swift smile lit Grim's face. Tilting his head, he leaned in and captured Leon's mouth in a deep, devouring kiss. He tasted of champagne and chocolate, tart and sweet blending on his tongue. Leon groaned, one hand tightening in Grim's hair and the other grabbing a handful of firm, cotton-clad ass. He loved the way Grim kissed. Nothing shy or tentative about it, not after that first time. Grim's kisses were always hungry and intense, even the quick little pecks he bestowed when they were just talking.

When Grim kissed, he meant it. Leon adored that about him.

"What do you want tonight?" Grim murmured, his breath warm on Leon's lips. "You want to fuck me? Or you want me to suck you?"

Pulling back with an effort, Leon smiled at Grim's lust-dazed expression. "Oh, no. Tonight's all about you. You tell me what you want, and I'll do it. Anything."

Grim blinked. "What?"

Chuckling, Leon swiped his thumb across Grim's lower lip. "I think you heard me."

Dropping his gaze so Leon couldn't see his eyes, Grim drew Leon's thumb into his mouth and sucked, his tongue rasping across the pad. Leon wasn't fooled by his soft little whimpers. Whenever Grim wanted to stall for time so he could think things through, he tried to distract Leon with his lips and tongue.

The sad thing was, it usually worked. Grim's mouth was pure magic, able to drive all rational thought from Leon's mind with a few flicks of his tongue even when it was just a thumb he was licking.

Leon managed to stay focused by reminding himself of how much Grim had endured in his short life, and how very much he deserved to have his body worshipped instead of abused.

Gently removing his thumb from Grim's mouth, Leon laid a hand on his cheek. "Listen to me, Grim. Tonight, what I want more than anything is to give you everything you ever wanted."

He raised Grim's chin and kissed him. "Tell me what you want, baby. The only thing I won't do is hurt you."

A strange blend of relief and disappointment crossed Grim's face and was gone before Leon could grasp it. Leon refused to let it bother him. He knew Grim wanted to play rough sometimes, but he didn't feel safe indulging that particular kink just yet. Maybe in a few more months, or a few more years, when John's influence had faded sufficiently for Leon to be certain it was Grim's desires talking, and not John's.

Grim opened his mouth, then closed it again. His cheeks flushed pink, his shoulders hunching.

"Say it," Leon urged, running his fingers through Grim's hair. "Whatever it is, you can tell me. I won't laugh, I won't think you're a freak, and I won't get angry. I promise. I just want to make you happy."

Grim stared at him, brown eyes huge and searching. Leon held his gaze without flinching. He meant every word he'd said, and was confident he could keep his promise.

"I...I like it when you lick me," Grim whispered. "You know, *there*."

It killed Leon that Grim could say the filthiest things when it came to asking what Leon wanted, but still spoke as if his own sexual needs were somehow wrong. Pulling Grim closer, Leon stuck one hand as far down the back of Grim's shorts as he could. "You want me to lick your asshole?" He slid a fingertip between Grim's buttocks. "You want me to eat you out? Fuck you with my tongue?"

A violent shudder ran through Grim's body. "It sounds so dirty when you say it like that."

"Nothing wrong with that. Dirty sex is fun." Dipping his head, Leon ran his tongue up Grim's throat. "You can say it, you know. You can tell me to eat your ass."

He'd given Grim countless rim jobs, knowing without being told how much Grim liked it. But he needed to hear Grim ask for it. More than that, *Grim* needed to know once and for all that he had the right to ask for what he needed.

Grim's breath ran out in a shaking sigh. His fingers dug into Leon's shoulder. "I want... Oh God."

"It's okay." Worming a hand between their bodies, Leon flipped open the button on Grim's shorts, tugged the zipper down as far as he could, and wriggled his fingers inside. He gently manipulated Grim's foreskin, at the same time shoving his other hand deeper into the back of Grim's shorts to rub light circles over his hole. Grim's resulting moan nearly had Leon coming in his pants. "Just say it, baby. Tell me. It's okay, I swear, just let me hear you say it for me."

Leon knew he was babbling, but he didn't care. The need to hear a purely selfish order from Grim's sweet lips was so strong his blood boiled with it. He latched his mouth onto Grim's shoulder and sucked, using his tongue to draw wet patterns on Grim's skin.

"Oh God," Grim gasped, trembling. "Leon. Fuck, eat me. Lick my ass."

That was all the invitation Leon needed. Pulling his hands out of Grim's shorts, he nudged the boy off his lap. "Lie down on your stomach."

Grim obeyed, folding his arms and laying his cheek on them. He gazed at Leon with smoldering eyes. "Take your clothes off first."

Oh, now *that* was hot. Grim ordering him to undress, his voice wavering slightly, but not hesitating at all. Once Grim made up his mind to do something, he didn't back down, even if he was afraid. Leon admired the hell out of him for that.

Leon climbed off the bed and started stripping. Shoes,

socks, jacket, holster, shirt. He made a show of pulling off his jeans and underwear, rotating his hips in a slow circle as he slid the garments down his thighs. He grinned at the naked lust in Grim's eyes. "Like what you see?"

Grim nodded. "Come back to bed now. Please?"

Leon elected not to mention the "please". One step at a time.

Abandoning his impromptu strip show, he kicked out of his jeans and boxer-briefs and crawled back onto the bed. He straddled Grim's body on all fours, bent and dug his teeth into the juncture of Grim's neck and shoulder.

Grim's back arched. "Oh. Leon."

Chuckling, Leon flicked his tongue over the flesh caught between his teeth. Mouthing that particular hot spot never failed to make Grim squirm in an agony of need, so of course Leon did it every chance he got.

Taking his time, Leon kissed and nipped his way down the length of Grim's spine. Each vertebra was lovingly caressed with lips and tongue, every inch of satin skin teased, touched and tasted. Grim's soft mewls and broken, incoherent pleas formed the perfect soundtrack for slow, languid lovemaking, and Leon hummed along as he explored Grim's body.

When he reached the small of Grim's back, Leon ran both palms over Grim's clothed ass, letting the anticipation build to an almost unbearable level. Grim whined and wriggled his backside against Leon's palms. "God, Leon, *please!*"

"Don't worry, beautiful." Leon curled his fingers around the waistband of Grim's shorts. "I'm gonna take care of you."

Grim let out a strangled sob as Leon tugged his shorts past the swell of his buttocks. "Leon. Oh, God."

Yanking the hideous shorts off, Leon tossed them on the

floor, pushed Grim's thighs apart and settled himself between them. He spread Grim's cheeks with his thumbs and buried his face in the damp crease, drawing a deep breath scented with musk and sweat. "Mmm. Fuck, I love your smell. Makes me so fucking hard." His tongue darted out, the tip teasing Grim's hole.

With a sharp cry, Grim bucked his hips upward, pressing his ass against Leon's face. Leon moved with him, riding the undulations of his body with an ease born of long practice. He'd never had a problem eating a guy's ass, but he fucking *loved* doing it to Grim. The way Grim lost all control, moaning and writhing in ecstasy, made Leon's spirit soar.

Once he felt the faint tremor in Grim's thighs which always signaled his impending orgasm, Leon stopped and drew back, forcing himself to ignore Grim's inarticulate protest. He licked his lips, gathering all he could of Grim's salty-sharp flavor.

"You want to come like this, baby? With my tongue up your ass?" Leon slid a finger into Grim's loose, slick hole, massaging the quivering ring of muscle. "Or you want my cock in there?" Adding a second finger, he twisted to rub Grim's gland. He basked in the resulting wanton groan like a cat in the sunshine. "Or maybe you want to fuck my mouth, and come down my throat." He leaned down and gently bit one firm, pale ass cheek. "Tell me how you want me to finish you, Grim."

Grim wailed, hands bunching the covers as Leon's fingers pumped in and out of him. "Oh God. Wanna fuck you."

Oh, shit. Leon went still, wondering if he'd heard wrong. "What? What'd you say?" The mental image of Grim's prick pounding into his ass had his cock pulsing and dripping on the bed. He wrapped his free hand around the base in an effort to stave off the rush of excitement which threatened to hurl him over the edge.

To Leon's dismay, Grim's entire body went tense. He dropped to the mattress, forcing Leon's fingers out of him, and curled into a ball. "N-nothing, I, I didn't mean it, I'm sorry." His face had lost the enticing flush of arousal and gone dead white, and his gaze wouldn't meet Leon's.

Silently cursing himself, Leon stretched out beside Grim and pulled him close. "Don't ever apologize to me for telling me what you want." He kissed Grim's forehead, his nose, each eyelid. "We're not always going to like the same things, but I don't want you to ever feel like you can't ask for what you want. Okay?"

Grim nodded, relaxing into Leon's embrace. "It's not easy for me," he murmured, acknowledging for the first time something Leon had known for ages. "But I'll try."

"Good." Leon rolled onto his back with his arms still around Grim, so that Grim ended up on top of him. He grinned at Grim's surprised expression. "You really want to fuck me?"

A charming blush colored Grim's cheeks. "Umm, yeah. I've never done that. I've been wondering what it feels like."

It had been a long, long time since Leon had bottomed for anyone—Ted had hated topping—but he didn't even have to think about his answer. As far as he was concerned, anything Grim wanted, Grim got. Besides, the thought of having Grim's cock inside him made him feel hot all over.

Leon parted his thighs so that Grim's groin nestled against his. "Okay."

Grim's eyebrows shot up. "Really?"

"Yeah, really." Leon tilted his hips up, rubbing his erection against Grim's and making them both groan. "It's been a while. We'll need to take it kind of slow."

"Slow. Yeah." Grim licked his lips. His eyes looked dazed. "Lube. We need lube."

Shoving a hand under the pillow behind him, Leon felt around until he found the new bottle of liquid lubricant he'd bought that afternoon. Grim snatched the bottle from Leon's hand, clicked the cap open and poured a generous amount into his palm. He sat back on his heels, staring at Leon with a solemn expression.

"Promise you'll tell me if I do something wrong," Grim said, stroking the inside of Leon's thigh with his dry palm. "I don't want to hurt you."

"You won't." Hooking his hands behind his knees, Leon pulled his legs up and apart, exposing himself completely to Grim. "One finger first. I'll tell you when I'm ready for more."

Brow furrowed in concentration, Grim rubbed one slippery fingertip against Leon's hole. Leon moaned at the feathery touch. Grim had never touched him in this most intimate of ways, not even once. He'd always assumed Grim just didn't want to. Plenty of men didn't. Looking back, however, he could see the truth about Grim's reluctance. It was John's "training" rearing its ugly head yet again. The signs were there. Leon just hadn't seen them.

Should've figured it was that bastard. Bet he thought his hole was fucking sacred.

It was Leon's last rational thought, before Grim's finger pressed inside him and all the blood left his brain.

"Yes, baby," Leon breathed, spreading himself open as much as he could. "Just like that. God."

Grim's wide-eyed gaze darted between Leon's face and his ass. "It's tight. And soft. Wow."

Grim caught his lower lip between his teeth. His finger slid in, out, in again, the movements slow and gentle and God, not enough.

Leon swallowed, licked his dry lips and managed to speak.

207

"'Nother one."

Grim's gaze darted up to meet Leon's. Sweat beaded on his brow and upper lip. Watching Leon's face, he worked a second finger in beside the first. "Is this okay? Leon?"

Leon was having trouble remembering how to talk. He forced himself to concentrate. "'S good. Move them—oh *fuck* yes, like that—move 'em apart. Twist. Oh."

He hoped to God Grim knew what he was trying to say, because he didn't think he could make it any clearer. His tongue felt thick and clumsy. The sensations spreading from his anus climbed vine-like up his spine to strangle all the sense out of his brain.

Luckily, Grim seemed to understand. Or maybe he just remembered how Leon had prepared him their first couple of times together. Either way, he was doing all the right things, twisting and scissoring his fingers as he pumped Leon's ass in a slow, steady motion.

Before long, Leon felt his muscles relax and loosen as his body remembered how to open up for a lover. Grim's long fingers went deeper, zinging over Leon's prostate. Liquid heat roared through Leon's body, making his toes curl.

"Jesus, Grim, now," Leon gasped, his vision blurring when Grim nailed his gland again. "Fuck, do it, fuck me!"

A tiny sound, somewhere between a growl and a whimper, bled from Grim's lips. Pulling his fingers out of Leon's hole, he picked up the lube bottle, opened it and drizzled some directly onto his rigid cock. His hands shook as he coated his shaft with the glistening liquid.

Slicked and ready, Grim tossed the lube aside, grasped his prick in one hand and laid the other on the back of Leon's thigh. He stared at Leon, looking young and scared. "I…I don't think it'll fit."

Leon let out a tight, breathy laugh. "It'll fit. Trust me."

Though he still looked a bit nervous, some of the fear melted from Grim's eyes, and he smiled. Warmth flowered in Leon's chest. *He really does trust me.* It was a wonderful feeling.

Dropping his gaze, Grim focused between Leon's legs with such intensity Leon could practically feel the heat of it. He moaned when he felt the tip of Grim's cock nudge his hole.

Grim leaned over until his face hovered over Leon's, strands of the hair he'd never bothered to cut brushing Leon's neck. His gaze boring into Leon's, Grim rocked his hips. There was a moment of resistance, then the head of his prick popped through Leon's entrance.

It burned, in spite of Grim's painstaking preparation. But Leon wouldn't have traded that sweet ache for anything. He had Grim inside him, and at that moment, life was perfect.

"Oh, my God." Grim's breath hitched. "So tight. Oh, Jesus, how... I c-can't... Fuck, I need to move, Leon, please, can I?"

Yes, fuck yes, move, move-move-move!

The words refused to come out. With a whine that would've embarrassed the hell out of him under other circumstances, Leon wrapped his legs around Grim's waist and lifted his hips. The movement forced Grim's cock deep inside him.

They both groaned. Beneath Leon's palms, Grim's back rippled. "Leon. God, so hot inside."

Snagging a handful of Grim's hair, Leon dragged his face down for a hard, open-mouthed kiss. "Fuck me," he growled. "Make me feel it."

Grim's lips moved, forming words Leon couldn't hear. Drawing a trembling breath, Grim pulled partway out of Leon's ass, then shoved back in. The head of his cock hit Leon's gland both ways, sending electric jolts along every nerve.

A strangled sob escaped Grim's throat. He dropped onto his elbows, his hair tickling Leon's cheek, and started thrusting hard.

During his teenage years and through his brief time in prison, Leon had been exclusively a bottom. Meeting Ted, falling in love with him, had changed all that. Leon had learned to top because Ted loved nothing better than being fucked through the floor. After a while, Leon had come to enjoy topping as much as Ted did bottoming. He hadn't missed being fucked in ages.

Until now.

Legs clamped around Grim, getting his ass pounded so hard his teeth rattled, Leon wondered if Grim would agree to top all the time.

Not that fucking Grim was any sort of hardship. Leon figured as long as he could spend the rest of his natural life in Grim's arms, he'd take the sex any way he could get it.

He felt Grim's excitement building, in the tremors running up and down his back and the little mewling noises he made. As always, the sight of Grim coming undone and the heady aroma of their mutual desire sent Leon's arousal spiraling tight inside him.

Reaching between them, Leon curled his fingers around his cock and started jerking himself off. He was close, so close, just a few more good pulls, a few more rough thrusts of Grim's cock...

Grim's weight shifted, and his hand shoved Leon's aside. Strong, slender fingers stroked Leon's prick hard and fast, twisting around the head just the way he liked. His back arched, one arm snaking around Grim's shoulders to dig into his sweat-soaked skin. Leon planted his other hand on the headboard behind him just in time to keep Grim's powerful thrusts from knocking his head against the carved oak.

"Close," Leon whimpered, staring up into Grim's eyes.

"Come," Grim panted. Sweat rolled down the side of his face and dripped onto Leon's cheek. "Want to see you come."

Grim's prick nailed Leon's gland, Grim's thumb caught the head of his cock, and Leon came with a jerk and a shout. His hole convulsed, his insides constricting around Grim's shaft. The air rang with Leon's cries. He clung to Grim, shaking and moaning while the orgasm thumped through him.

Inside him, Grim's cock swelled and pulsed. His rhythm degenerated into mindless rutting, rough and graceless, and Leon knew he was on the edge. Fascinated as always, Leon watched the telltale furrow appear between Grim's brows and listened to the sweet familiar noises Grim made when he was about to come.

"Grim..." Taking his hand off the headboard and tightening the clutch of his legs around Grim's waist, Leon reached up to touch Grim's flushed and sweaty face. "So beautiful, baby, come on, come inside me, fill me up."

As if in answer to Leon's babbling, Grim threw his head back and wailed as he came, his cock buried deep in Leon's ass. Leon could've sworn he actually felt the hot spurt of Grim's semen inside him, even though he knew it was probably his imagination.

Grim stayed there for a long moment, his body tense and trembling, before collapsing in a heap on top of Leon. His breath came in gasps, and his heart hammered against Leon's chest. Leon held him close, stroking his back and damp hair.

With Grim in his arms, face tucked into the curve of his neck and cock still twitching in his ass, Leon felt a wonderful sense of peace wash through him. This, he thought, was what life was all about. Lying in bed, naked and sweaty from mind-blowing sex, curled up with the man he loved.

Speaking of which, this seemed like the perfect time to give Grim his last gift. The most special one of all.

God, I hope it doesn't freak him out.

Brushing the hair from Grim's face, Leon kissed his brow. "You good, baby?"

"Mmm-hmm." Grim stretched, causing his softening prick to slip out of Leon's body. He hissed as the head popped free. "Oh, damn. Sensitive."

Leon chuckled, causing Grim's spunk to seep out of his hole and puddle on the brand new comforter beneath his butt. He squirmed against the sticky tickle. "So what'd you think of topping? You like it?"

"Definitely. It's amazing." Grim raised his head, giving Leon a lazy, sated smile. "I never thought anything could feel as good as you fucking me, but I think this comes awfully close."

"Good. We'll take turns." Pressing a quick kiss to Grim's lips, Leon unlocked his legs from around Grim's waist. "Let me up. I have something for you."

Grim's eyebrows went up. "Another present?" He rolled to the side, flopping onto his back with a sigh. "God, I feel like an overcooked noodle. I don't think I can move."

"Don't, then. I'll bring you your present right here." Leon heaved himself to a sitting position, scooted to the edge of the bed and stood. He grimaced at the spunk trickling down his leg. "Let me just get a washcloth first."

Snickering, Grim tucked a hand behind his head and bent his knees up, planting both feet on the mattress. "I hate when it runs out like that."

"Yeah, I'd forgotten that part. I'll take it, though, if it means getting your cock up my ass on a regular basis."

Leon walked rather gingerly to the bathroom, followed by

Grim's laughter. The wonderful soreness from a good fucking was something else he'd forgotten.

Spotting a dry washcloth crumpled beside the sink, Leon picked it up and perused it with a critical eye. It seemed clean enough. He soaked it in warm water, rang it out and scrubbed the coagulating semen from his ass and thighs. Tossing the cloth on the floor beside the tub, he grabbed a fresh one from the linen closet and dampened it for Grim.

Back in the bedroom, Grim lay with his eyes half closed and lips slightly parted. Leon went to him, leaned down and flicked his tongue over that sweet, kiss-swollen mouth. "Here. I brought you a cloth too."

Grim took it with a smile. "Thanks." He gazed thoughtfully at Leon while he swabbed his genitals. "I always liked this about you."

"What?" Leon sat on the bed and rummaged behind the pile of books Grim kept on the lower shelf of the bedside table for the box he'd hidden there earlier. "My devastating good looks? My perfect ass? My monster cock? What'd you like?"

Giggling, Grim punched Leon in the shoulder. "Are you fishing for compliments?"

"Always." Retrieving the box, Leon hid it in his palm.

Grim sat up and kissed the red spot where he'd hit Leon. "You're the hottest thing going, you have a perfect ass, and your cock's fucking huge. Yeah, I like that."

"Liar. Flattery'll get you laid." Leon waggled his eyebrows.

Grim laughed again, and bit Leon's upper arm. "I always liked that you let me wash off. I took a chance that first time, you know. You just seemed like you wouldn't mind. Then you wanted to know what I was doing, and I thought you were mad because I got up to wash." Moving closer, Grim laid his head on Leon's shoulder. "John never let me wash off. He said he liked

213

watching his come run out of my ass. I'm glad you let me clean it off. It just makes me think of him whenever it runs down my leg, and I don't want to think of him."

A familiar anger dug its teeth into Leon's gut. Privately, he'd always found the sight of his spunk dribbling from Grim's asshole incredibly sexy. Damned if he'd ever think so again. He resented John for that.

Fuck you, John. Fucking with us even after you're dead.

Slipping the little black velvet box underneath the pillow and hoping Grim didn't notice, Leon put both arms around Grim and held him tight. "You don't need me to *let* you do anything, Grim. You know that, right?"

"I know. It's just hard to not think that way, after so long. But I'm trying." Raising his head, Grim pinned Leon with a solemn stare. "John made me do a lot of things I never wanted. He tried to make me think I was a thing for him to keep, not a person. I know that now."

It was the one thing Leon had longed to hear ever since he'd first figured out he was falling in love with Grim. Happiness swelled in Leon's chest, cutting off any words he might've said. He captured Grim's mouth in a deep kiss which said all the things he didn't know how to.

"Mmm," Grim hummed when they broke apart several minutes later. "So."

"So what?" Leon nipped Grim's chin. Damned if his cock wasn't starting to stir again.

"So, what'd you hide under the pillow?"

Here we go. Leon sat back, his pulse racing with a sudden attack of nerves. He grinned. "Go ahead and take it out."

Grim shot Leon a reproachful look as he groped under the pillow. "You shouldn't have gotten me all this stuff."

Leon wasn't fooled. Grim's eyes shone like a kid's on Christmas morning. "I wanted to. What good's being rich if you can't spend the money on cool stuff?"

Shaking his head, Grim pulled the box from beneath the pillow. His smile faded, all the color draining from his face. He looked up, his expression radiating shock. "Leon?"

Leon licked his lips. He didn't think he'd ever been this nervous in his life. "Open it."

Grim looked down at the box in his palm. He stroked a finger over the top, as if he was afraid it might not be real. Just when Leon thought he might explode from suspense, Grim lifted the lid and peered inside. His mouth fell open. "Oh. Oh, my God."

Wanting more than anything to touch Grim, but afraid to do it right now, Leon clasped his hands in his lap. "Do you like it?"

Grim didn't answer, just stared into the box like he'd been hypnotized. Leon waited, mouth dry and heart galloping like a race horse. *Fuck, it's too soon, Fisher, you asshole, you fucked it all up. Fuck!*

"It's the most beautiful thing I've ever seen," Grim said, his voice soft and reverent. He lifted the thick gold band from the box and held it up. It gleamed in the candlelight. "It's for me? Really?"

The look in Grim's eyes was hopeful, but flinching, as if he was afraid Leon would tell him it was all a joke. It made Leon ache inside to see that look.

Reaching over, Leon took the ring and angled it so Grim could see the inscription on the inside. "Of course it's for you. See?"

Grim squinted at the tiny letters. "For Grim, from Leon," he read, sounding the words with painstaking precision. "All my

215

love, always." He turned his wide, startled eyes to Leon. "You love me?"

Leon nodded. "I've loved you for a long time now." The admission wasn't as difficult as Leon had expected it to be. He smiled, pleased with himself for having said the words finally.

To his relief, Grim's face broke into a huge, childlike smile. Grabbing the back of Leon's head, he yanked him forward and kissed him hard. "I love you too," he whispered. "But I bet you knew that."

"I hoped so." Leon laughed, dispelling the last of his tension. "Here, give me your hand."

Grim obediently held out his hand. Leon slid the ring onto his fourth finger. It was a perfect fit. The gold seemed to shine brighter now that it lay against Grim's skin.

Beaming, Grim threw his arms around Leon's neck in a bone-cracking hug. "Thank you, Leon. I love it. I love everything, this whole evening. Thank you."

Leon ran his hands up and down Grim's bare back, savoring the feel of warm skin and hard muscle. "Like I said before, you deserve it."

Grim drew back, looking stricken. "Leon, I didn't get you anything. I'm sorry."

"I knew you'd say that." Smiling, Leon took Grim's hand and kissed his knuckles. The ring, heated by Grim's skin, felt warm against his lips. "You give me the best gift there is every day, just by being here. I don't need anything else."

It sounded sappy, but Leon didn't care. Every word was true. Besides, the pure joy on Grim's face made any amount of sappiness worthwhile.

Grim reached over and grabbed the champagne from the bedside table. He squirmed onto Leon's lap, the bottle clutched in one hand. "Let's drink the rest of this insanely expensive booze before it goes flat, then fuck some more."

"I like that plan." Taking the Cristal from Grim's hand, Leon took a long swallow straight from the bottle. "But what if we can't get it up? Alcohol's a depressant."

Grim shrugged. "If we can't, we can't." He pulled the bottle from Leon's hand and drank. "It doesn't matter. I just like being with you like this."

Leon's throat went tight. No one had ever said anything like that to him before. Not even Ted. Leon realized, with a pleasant shock, that he'd never felt as comfortable—as *safe*—with anyone as he did with Grim.

Burying a hand in Grim's hair, Leon kissed his champagne-flavored lips. "Grim?"

"Hmm?" The tip of Grim's tongue traced Leon's upper lip.

"Put down that bottle."

Epilogue

Some hours later, Leon lay wide awake, staring at the ceiling. His brain was going ninety miles a second and he couldn't sleep. He felt restless and fidgety.

Might as well get up, before you wake Grim up too.

Moving as carefully as he could, Leon disentangled himself from Grim's sleeping embrace and slipped out of the bed. Grim mumbled something unintelligible, rolled onto his stomach and lay still.

For a moment Leon just stood there, looking at Grim. He had one arm under his pillow and the other curled beneath his chin. His hair was in knots, his lips still red and swollen from the evening's celebration. One bent knee stuck out of the tangle of sheets wound around his hips.

Leon thought he'd never laid eyes on a more enticing sight. Bending down, he pressed his lips to Grim's cheek. Grim smelled of sweat, sex and champagne. Best scent in the world, in Leon's opinion.

Naked, he padded into the living room and stood gazing at the stretch of grass sloping from the house to the eaves of the forest. A brilliant half-moon hung above the trees, washing the scene in silvery light.

It was so quiet here. So peaceful. Leon loved having a thriving city nearby, but he needed the sanctuary this place offered. Here, it was just Grim and Leon, alone in their own private corner of the world. Leon's money kept them fed, clothed and housed in luxury, and Vancouver and the surrounding wilderness offered all the entertainment any man could want. He and Grim had no stress here, no worry. Their lives couldn't have been more perfect.

So why, Leon wondered, was he standing at the living room window at three in the morning instead of sleeping the sleep of the well-fucked like Grim was?

He didn't understand his restlessness, when his life these past few months had resembled the ending of one of Grim's Happily Ever After romances. Grim had made huge strides in accepting—and therefore learning to get past—his sad and abusive history. Leon had eventually accepted Grim's word that John was dead, and had let go of the useless desire for revenge. Grudgingly, true, but he'd let it go, and felt better for having done so. It seemed that Jones' employers had even given up hunting them. At least, that's what Melissa had heard from her contacts closest to the organization's core, and Melissa's information had always been rock solid. Though he still carried his gun everywhere and still kept one eye out for signs of pursuit, he'd ceased to seriously worry about it months ago.

No worry. None.

The revelation hit him like a two by four to the gut. He put a hand out to steady himself.

"That's it," he whispered to the raccoon ambling across the grass outside. "There's nothing to worry about anymore. Nothing."

All his life, Leon had lived with varying degrees of stress, tension and anger. Even during his years with Ted, there had been the nonstop vigilance inherent in his line of work. Now, for the first time, he felt perfectly centered and at peace with himself. There was still a vague ache inside him when he thought of Ted and the brutal way he'd died, but it no longer had the power to paralyze Leon with sorrow and rage.

I'm happy, Leon thought, with a sense of awe. *Really, truly happy, with nothing in the way.*

The feeling was unfamiliar enough that it echoed in Leon's brain, keeping him from resting. Now that he recognized it, though, he figured he could get used to it. He'd sure as hell like to try.

Sensing sleep creeping up on him, Leon wandered back to the bedroom. He straightened the covers as best he could and crawled in beside Grim, who promptly wound arms and legs around him.

"Where'd you go?" Grim murmured, settling his head on Leon's chest.

"Nowhere. Just looking out the window for a minute." Brushing the hair from Grim's face, Leon kissed his brow. "Go back to sleep, baby. Sorry I woke you up."

"Mm-kay."

Grim burrowed his face into the curve of Leon's neck and was asleep again in seconds, his breathing deep and even. Smiling, Leon rested his cheek against Grim's head and shut his eyes.

When he drifted to sleep, with Grim still wrapped tight in his arms, he didn't dream.

About the Author

Ally Blue used to be a good girl. Really. Married for twenty years, two lovely children, house, dogs, picket fence, the whole deal. Then one day she discovered slash fan fiction. She wrote her first fan fiction story a couple of months later and has since slid merrily into the abyss. She has had several short stories published in the erotic e-zine Ruthie's Club, and is a regular contributor to the original slash e-zine Forbidden Fruit.

To learn more about Ally Blue, please visit www.allyblue.com. Send an email to Ally at ally@allyblue.com or join her Yahoo! group to join in the fun with other readers as well as Ally! http://groups.yahoo.com/group/loveisblue/.

When Sam Raintree goes to work for Bay City Paranormal Investigations, he expects his quiet life to change—he doesn't expect to put his life and sanity on the line, or to fall for a man he can never have.

Oleander House
© 2006 Ally Blue
Book One in the Bay City Paranormal Investigation series.

Sam Raintree has never been normal. All his life, he's experienced things he can't explain. Things that have colored his view of the world and of himself. So taking a job as a paranormal investigator seems like a perfect fit. His new co-workers, he figures, don't have to know he's gay.

When Sam arrives at Oleander House, the site of his first assignment with Bay City Paranormal Investigations, nothing is what he expected. The repetitive yet exciting work, the unusual and violent history of the house, the intensely erotic and terrifying dreams which plague his sleep. But the most unexpected thing is Dr. Bo Broussard, the group's leader.

From the moment they meet, Sam is strongly attracted to his intelligent, alluring boss. It doesn't take Sam long to figure out that although Bo has led a heterosexual life, he is very much in the closet, and wants Sam as badly as Sam wants him.

As the investigation of Oleander House progresses and paranormal events in the house escalate, Sam and Bo circle warily around their mutual attraction, until a single night of bloodshed and revelation changes their lives forever.

Warning: this title contains explicit male/male sex, intense violence, and graphic language.

Available now in ebook and print from Samhain Publishing.

Jackson knows he needs protection from a stalker, but the last thing he wants is to want his bodyguard.

Court Appointed
© 2008 Annmarie McKenna
A Serving Love story.

After receiving several suspicious "gifts", His Honor Jackson Benedict is assigned an agent for protection. He'd be fine with a bodyguard…if he was anyone but the man who enters his courtroom looking hotter than any man has a right to look. Thank God Jackson's robe hides his interest.

Trey London is more than happy that Jackson has practically been handed to him on a silver platter. If his job requires he stay close to one of the country's youngest federal judges, it's no skin off his back. The closer the better, actually.

But someone else is getting closer, too, and when the gifts turn into attacks, Trey is forced to trade his status of new lover for that of protector. He's not about to let anyone come between him and his judge.

Warning, this title contains the following: explicit, nekkid, sometimes robed, m/m judge on bodyguard sex, and graphic language.

Available now in ebook and in the print Serving Love from Samhain Publishing.

Lightning Source UK Ltd.
Milton Keynes UK
11 November 2009

146115UK00001B/167/P